The Ultimate Christmas Gift

Best friends, a surrogate baby, and a chance for love…

Best friends Emma Hayes and Abbie Cook will do *anything* for each other. So when nurse Abbie asks Emma if she'll be her surrogate and carry the baby she longs for, of course she doesn't refuse.

But as Christmas comes, it's not just the new baby that turns their lives upside down. Because for both women there's a chance for love…if they're only brave enough to take it!

Read Abbie and Callum's story in
The Nurse's Special Delivery

And discover Emma and Nixon's story in
Her New Year Baby Surprise

Both available now!

Dear Reader,

When the Medical Romance editors suggested Sue MacKay and I write another duet (our first was The Infamous Maitland Brothers with *The Gift of a Child* and *How to Resist a Heartbreaker*), I was thrilled. Sue and I had a lot of fun the first time around and I knew we'd have the same on our second duet.

Writing *The Nurse's Special Delivery* gave me the chance to share my love of Queenstown on New Zealand's South Island, one of my very favorite places in the world. It's a stunningly beautiful place; a town on the edge of a deep blue lake surrounded by snow-capped mountains. The area is a tourist haven and renowned for its sense of fun and adventure. I hope both Sue and I captured a bit of that in these stories, too.

In this duet we've taken a few risks and covered a topic that is not often talked about; surrogacy. Abbie can't carry her own child so her best friend Emma offers to do it for her in a completely unselfish act that embodies what their friendship has meant over twenty years. These two brave, compassionate and feisty women need strong heroes and we definitely found them in Callum and Nixon!

Callum has enough demons of his own and is only visiting New Zealand for a short time. He does not need or want to fall in love with a place and a woman and he definitely cannot imagine himself being a father to someone else's baby. Meanwhile, Abbie is preparing for her first child and has no time or space in her life for a man. So, the road to love is a rocky one with both parties resisting all the way!

I hope you enjoy Callum and Abbie's story!

Best wishes,

Louisa xx

THE NURSE'S
SPECIAL DELIVERY

—

LOUISA GEORGE

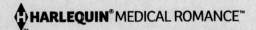

Recycling programs for this product may not exist in your area.

ISBN-13: 978-0-373-21572-0

The Nurse's Special Delivery

First North American Publication 2017

Copyright © 2017 by Louisa George

Printed in U.S.A.

Books by Louisa George

Harlequin Medical Romance

The Hollywood Hills Clinic
Tempted by Hollywood's Top Doc

Midwives On-Call at Christmas
Her Doctor's Christmas Proposal

One Month to Become a Mom
Waking Up With His Runaway Bride
The War Hero's Locked-Away Heart
The Last Doctor She Should Ever Date
How to Resist a Heartbreaker
200 Harley Street: The Shameless Maverick
A Baby on Her Christmas List
Tempted by Her Italian Surgeon

Visit the Author Profile page
at Harlequin.com for more titles.

PROLOGUE

THE SOUND OF tinkling bells and Christmas carols floated into Abbie Cook's head. Followed by laughter. Hungry newborns grizzling. The chink of teacups. The smell of coffee that still made her nauseous.

Go away, world.

The babies' cries felt as if they had a direct line to her heart, tugging and stabbing and shaping it into a raw lump of pain. She kept her eyes tightly closed as she focused on keeping the contents of her stomach precisely where they were.

'Merry Christmas, Abbie. Wake up, the doctor's going to do his rounds in a minute. You might be able to go home. You'll want to be home, dear, on Christmas Day, won't you?'

Even though her eyes were clamped shut, Abbie felt the slide of the tear down her cheek and she turned away from the nurse's voice. The last thing she wanted was to go home to that empty house with an empty belly and a completely cried-out heart. Staying asleep, hibernating under the regulation hospital duvet, was just perfect, especially today.

Her third Christmas without Michael. The first had been a blur of condolence messages. The second a pretence of fun with people who *didn't think she should be alone*, when all she'd wanted was to be alone. And now this. Another year without decorations, another year gone by, without keeping her promise to her husband.

But it didn't do to feel sorry for herself on a ward in the hospital she worked in. There'd been enough pity glances from her colleagues these past few weeks. Actually, years. And enough self-pity too. What would Michael think of her? He wouldn't have wanted her to feel like this, that was for sure. He'd have wanted her to get up and make the most of her life regardless of what befell her. He'd want her to keep on fighting for happiness. He'd have wanted her to decorate the house, to celebrate Christmas and enjoy life.

She heaved herself up the bed and looked at the cup of steaming tea, hoping the well-meaning staff nurse would do a bunk and leave her on her own. 'Thanks. Yeah. Okay.'

'Hey, love.' A hand slid over hers. 'You'll be okay. You will—'

'Abbie! Abbie! Santa Claus been!'

'Uh-huh. Visitors.' The nurse's hand shrugged

off as thudding footsteps sliced through the
ward's white noise and a giggling, wriggling
four-year-old scrambled onto the bed thrust-
ing a box with sharp edges into Abbie's hands.
'Abbie! Look.'

'Hey, Scratch. Let me see.' It was hard to be
sad around Rosie, who grasped her life with tight
little fists and squeezed out every drop of every
second. Abbie took the box and peered. 'What
have you got here?'

'A tablet. For games and writing.' As the little girl spoke her dark curls bobbed from side to
side and the tiny, jaded bit left of Abbie's heart
squeezed.

'Oh. Lovely.' Abbie glanced up at Rosie's
mum, Emma, and pigged her eyes. 'A tablet.
Okay. Excellent?'

'Apparently the best present. In the world.
Someone didn't realise I was holding off until
she was older.' Emma gave a resigned shrug as
she perched on the bed—against all hospital
policies—but Abbie loved her for it. And she
assumed *someone* referred to one of Emma's
brothers who overcompensated for Rosie's lack
of a father. At least this year he hadn't bought
her another football. 'How are you doing, hun?'

Abbie dug very deep. It was Christmas Day.
She wasn't going to spoil it for a four-year-old.
'Fine, thanks.'

'You look better.'

'Yeah. I'm okay.' She lowered her voice a little to prevent little listening ears from hearing. 'I've been thinking. A lot.'

'Me too!' There was a light in Emma's eyes that melded with the ever-present sadness that was there whenever she was around Abbie. She'd seen that sadness before, too, when Emma had been having her own troubles. 'You first—'

'You first!'

'Jinx!' Abbie laughed for the first time in what felt like forever. That was the thing about best friends—after almost twenty years of living in each other's pockets they finished sentences and had a strange and comforting telepathy. 'Okay. If you don't mind, I'm just going to say something and I want you to be honest. Okay?'

'Okay.' As she nodded Emma absent-mindedly stroked her daughter's curls. A simple action that was feral and instinctive and that Abbie craved to do to a child of her own with every atom in her body.

'Okay.' She sat a little straighter. 'The thing is, I can't do this any more. God, I want to; I want a baby more than anything in the world, you know that. But Dr Morrison was frank—I can't carry one to term. Ever. I've tried and tried and it's not going to happen. I can't put myself through that again so I have to face up to it. I can't have

Michael's baby. I will never have it.' Her throat felt raw and her stomach tightened. It was reality and she had to deal with it. 'So. There it is. I'm not going to try *one more time* again. No more hormones or injections. No more baby books. Or bootees.' And now she was just being over-sentimental.

Emma's lip wobbled a little. 'Oh, honey, I'm so sorry. I really am.'

'I haven't been ready to stop for so long. I just wasn't ready to let go. I'm not sure if I really am, but I do have to accept that my husband is dead. That I won't be having his baby, because…because I just can't.' Abbie's chest felt as if it had a thick weight pressing on it. 'I tried. God knows, I tried.'

Twisting the edge of the duvet in her fingers, she rallied. 'So, I'm moving on. I'm going to leave NICU because I just can't face working with those little ones every day. I don't know what I'm going to do, but I'm determined that this time next year I'm going to be in a new job. At least, maybe my career can be my baby instead? That's something to look forward to, right? I've actually made the decision to let go. It hurts like hell, but…' Actually, it felt like a betrayal for everything she'd promised Michael, for everything they'd worked towards. She was betraying him and it felt like a knife in her heart.

But… 'Anyway, no more hormones, so that's a relief. Well, happy Christmas to me. I may even put a tree up next year too. Who knows? Oh, and I got you both a present but they're at home. Right. What do you think?'

'Oh, honey, I know what it's taken for you to say that. I think you need a break and some rest and some time.' Emma wrapped her in a hug. 'But it is lovely to see you being positive.'

Abbie blew out a long sigh. 'Okay, so you don't think I'm giving up too easily? Good. Thanks. So, what do you have to tell me?'

'Rosie, love… Let me show you how to do this. Look, you can draw pictures…' Emma sat her daughter on a chair and gave her the little tablet device. After promising she wouldn't let technology become a babysitter, maybe she was learning it could be a good distraction tool for a few minutes. 'Okay, Abbie. I've been doing a lot of soul-searching. I…don't actually know how to say this…' Emma laughed nervously. 'I want to do something for you. Nursing a husband through cancer is bad enough, but losing baby after baby was killing you. And I love that you want a new job and everything instead of a baby and that you're trying to be brave, but I also know that that's something you've always dreamt about since we were little. You'd be a fabulous mum. You of all people deserve to have a baby—yours and Michael's. So…' Emma slipped her hand over Abbie's. 'I want to have it for you.'

'You…what?' Joy swam across Abbie's chest, swiftly followed by panic and anxiety and…well, guilt and shame that she couldn't do this herself. But, immense gratitude. And hope. Yes, hope fluttering in her chest—it was strange to feel something like this after so long. 'You want to have a baby for me? What? How?'

'I want to be the surrogate, the oven. I'll cook your baby.' Emma's eyes narrowed and she looked a little panicked now too. 'Is that a really bad idea? It's okay. I just thought—'

Her baby. Michael's baby. Carried to term. Their baby. A precious tiny gift. 'But there's so much… I don't know… It's a surprise. It's a miracle.'

'A good one?'

'Oh, yes! Oh, yes! Thank you. I can't even… I just don't know what to say. Wow. How? I don't know…'

'Ways and means. Let me do this for you, please. I've seen the way you look at Rosie and it breaks my heart that you have so much love to give. You've been with me every step of the way through the good and the bad and…' Emma smiled softly over at her daughter and Abbie knew she was referring to Rosie's dad '…and the very ugly. You've been my rock and now I want to be yours. Please say yes.'

Abbie's heart felt as if it would explode. But there were so many questions running through her head too. How would she feel with her baby inside someone else? What would they tell other people? Rosie? Would she understand? Would their families?

What if you change your mind?

Surrogates did. And battles started. Friendships broke. She shoved that away. That would never happen. Their friendship was tight, and, oh, what a gift. A baby. 'Yes! Yes. If that's what you want. Yes. I'd love it. Oh, my God! Imagine! Thank you. Thank you so much. I love you to bits.'

'Yeah, you'll do too. Oh, and happy Christmas.' More tears glistened in Emma's eyes. Commitment shone through, and love, as she hugged her again for the zillionth time in twenty-odd years. 'Excellent. Right then, let's get cooking.'

CHAPTER ONE

Ten and a half months later...

'Er... I THINK we're having an alien.'

'Or a windmill. Look at those arms and legs moving.'

Trying to make out the shapes on the black and white screen was getting easier the further the pregnancy progressed. Today, they could see the baby in its entirety, filling the screen, all the features as clear as day. A stubby nose. *Like Michael's?* The bow lips. *Mine?* The rapid-fire heartbeat filled the room. *Wow.*

With a mix of sadness and epic excitement Abbie blinked back tears and squeezed her friend's hand. 'Oops, it's pass-the-tissues time. I'm being such a wuss, but I just can't believe it's real.'

'You've said that at every scan and every appointment. And a million times every day since the positive test. Not believing it's real hasn't stopped you shopping up a storm, though.' Laughing, Emma patted her swollen belly. 'Should we find out the gender?'

The sonographer looked up from the scanner screen. 'You want to know?'

'No. No.' It didn't feel right for some reason. Abbie stared at the screen and convinced herself the images weren't that clear really. She wasn't ready to hear she was having a mini-Michael. When she thought about him she wished he were here with her, getting all gooey about their child. He should have been here, holding her hand. Hell, she should have been the pregnant one, not Emma. But life hadn't granted her all the wishes she'd had and everything was happening out of sync. Suddenly, she felt a little deflated. 'Let's leave it as a surprise. Is that okay, Em?'

'Hey…it's your baby, after all.' Emma grinned and Abbie just knew her friend was watching to see the sonographer's reaction. The story of their baby was pretty unusual; surrogacy wasn't something they came across every day in little old Queenstown. 'Anyway, I think I know what sex it is and I bet I'm right. I'm one of those people who knows they're pregnant before the test shows up positive, and I'm convinced I know the gender because I'm carrying in a particular way. But my lips are sealed.'

'The main thing,' Abbie ventured, because this

was a question continually on her lips, in her thoughts—and after everything that had happened, who could blame her for having just the odd nugget of panic? 'Is everything okay?'

'Absolutely fine.'

'Are you sure?'

'Here's a picture for you both so you can see just how perfect baby is.' The sonographer smiled. 'I'll sort you out a DVD too. Yes, Abbie, baby is doing just fine for thirty-four weeks. And Mum…er…sorry, *Emma* is doing great too.'

Awkward. But it wasn't the first time and it probably wouldn't be the last.

Emma wiped the jelly off her belly and sat up. 'I feel great. And don't worry, we get that a lot. Okay, missy, you'd better get back to work, right? Busy day?'

Emma was always so chirpy at these appointments—and every day in between—laughing and joking, but she'd been here before when she was pregnant with Rosie. How was she really feeling, though? Did she feel like the mum this time too? Would she be bereft at handing the baby over? Would she want to keep the baby herself?

'Abbie?'

'Oh. Sorry.' Abbie glanced at the wall clock and pushed back the little, silly anxieties she had—of course Emma was going to hand this baby over. 'Oh, yes. My lunch break has finished. Gotta dash. See you later. Enjoy the rest of your day off.'

'I have a few hours before I pick Rosie up from school. Do you want me to get any shopping in for you?'

Abbie gave her friend a hug. 'No. I'm good, thanks—do you want me to sort dinner out? No—let's have a quick coffee before we pick her up. Meet in the staff canteen? We can talk shopping and dinner then. Listen to us, we're like an old couple.'

'No man's got a chance.' Emma laughed again, but there was more than a kernel of truth in her words. 'No complications. Just how I like it.'

Just how they both liked it, really. Between them they'd had a rough ride where relationships were concerned. One husband dead, the other might as well have been, for all the good he was. After all the heartbreak they'd had, who needed another man?

As Abbie walked down the corridor towards the emergency department and the rest of her shift, she thought about how things had changed. Eight years with one man who'd been her life completely, then three years in the wilderness. But she was fine about it. No man would come close to Michael. She would bring this baby up on her own, in his memory... Or as much on her own as her next-door-neighbour-best-friend-for-life would allow.

As she turned the corner into the department she heard voices.

'Imagine if someone you loved couldn't have a baby, and you knew you could. Would you do it? For a friend? A sister? Would you have a baby for someone else? It's a long nine months, though, isn't it? What if something went wrong? What if they decided they didn't want it, what then?'

Another voice in a stage whisper that echoed around the quieter than usual emergency department replied, 'Honestly, I don't know how a mother could give her baby away. All those months inside her, kicking, hiccups, little feet under your ribs…you have a bond, y'know? You're not telling me that you don't develop a bond. It's living inside you.' There was a pause where Abbie imagined the gossipers all shaking their heads. Then… 'Oh. Er… Hello, Abbie. We…er…hello.'

'Hi.' She was standing where she'd frozen to the spot the second she'd heard the subject of their conversation, probably looking like a complete idiot with her mouth open and bright red cheeks. Her hand was still clutching the scan picture. Her heart was raging. Raging with all the things she wanted to tell them, but it was none of their business.

How she'd wanted to feel the kicks and the hiccups, but no pregnancy had ever progressed past fifteen weeks. How many times she'd had IVF. How many times she'd failed. Until she hadn't had the energy to do it any more and keep on failing.

It's my baby. Not Emma's.

Made with my eggs and Michael's frozen sperm. It's our baby. Just a different incubator.

It wasn't as if she hadn't been over and over and over these thoughts every day since the minute a grinning, glowing Emma had shown her the pregnancy stick with the positive blue line. She'd loved her friend in that moment more than she'd loved anyone else ever—possibly even more than Michael—for doing something so precious. And she would love this baby as fiercely, no matter what. Finally, she'd have a family—a family of two. Other single parents managed, Emma did, so she would too. Just the two of them in a tight little unit.

And she'd always known she'd be the subject of gossip. How could she not be? Surrogacy wasn't common and people needed educating, otherwise the stigma would be with her baby for life. She gave them all a smile. 'If I could do it for someone else, I honestly would. I just can't even do it for me, which is why Emma's helping me out. She says to think of her as being the oven, but the bun is made from my ingredients. Does that make sense?'

There was a moment where they all gaped back at her, as open-mouthed as she'd been, and she hoped her message was getting through.

'Of course, Abbie, it makes perfect sense. Now, back to work everyone.' Stephanie, Head Nurse of Queenstown ED, and very well respected for her no-nonsense approach, turned to the group, thankfully distracting Abbie from the conversation topic and the need to defend herself. No one could possibly understand what she and Emma were going through—and that was fine.

With a few words from their boss, the subject of Abbie's baby's parentage and unconventional conception was closed. For now.

Thank you.

'Wait, Abbie. There's a Code Two call, and I want you to go with the helo. Tramper took a bad fall on Ben Lomond.'

'A medivac? On the helicopter?' Excitement bubbled in her stomach and she pushed all her baggage to the back of her mind. Four months in and she still couldn't get over the adrenalin rush of working at the coalface that was emergency medicine. Every day, every second, was different from the last, with no idea of what she might have to deal with next.

'We've got enough staff to cover, so yes. This

is your chance to watch and learn what it's like out in the field.'

'Sure thing.' Abbie controlled the fluttering in her chest. 'Thanks, Steph.'

'No problem.' Her boss smiled and said in a voice that everyone would hear, 'For the record, how you choose to have your child is no one's business but yours and I think it's wonderful. Put me down for babysitting duties. Now, out you go.'

It was the beginning of spring, so theoretically Queenstown should have been warming up from the previous long cold months, but there was still a good dusting of snow on the tops of the mountains and a cruel wind whipped across the helipad, liberating Abbie's unruly mane from the clips and elastic that were supposed to hold it all in place. Really, longer length was theoretically easier to look after but would she get a mum's bob when the baby came? Her heart thrilled a little at the thought, and she laughed at the image in her head of her being all mumsy with a short, neat, practical bob, at the thought of being a mumsy mummy after so long trying.

She was trying to fix the wayward hair neatly back under control when a chopper's chugging split the air. No time for vanity.

What am I supposed to do?

She ran through the protocols in her head and

hoped she'd remember them under stress. But the Intensive Care Paramedics and crew knew what they were doing; she'd learnt that much over the last few months. She'd met them all and been impressed with every one so far.

Soon enough the chopper door slid open and a man dressed in bright red paramedic dungarees jumped down. Shane, the town's senior paramedic and old family friend, wrapped her in a hug, said something she couldn't hear over the chopper blades and bundled her towards the helicopter.

Through the open door she could see more crew. Oh. A new one. He had a shock of dark hair. Celtic colouring, like her late grandad. Irish heritage, maybe? Perfect skin. Blue eyes. Nice mouth. A smattering of stubble, which made him look rugged and a little dangerous.

Back to his eyes—because she wanted to take a second look—they really were quite the brightest of blues, like the Queenstown sky on a crisp winter morning.

Where the hell had that thought come from?

Mr Nice Eyes raised his eyebrows as he met her gaze. Out of nowhere she felt a strange fluttery feeling in her stomach.

A medivac! Exciting! She was moving up in the world!

Shane coughed, nudging her forward, and she

drew her eyes away from the new guy. Now... what the hell was she supposed to do?

With the touchdown being as choppy as a protein shake in a blender, Intensive Care Paramedic Callum Baird's stomach had been left somewhere ten metres above Queenstown hospital. He breathed in the rush of cold air blasting through the open door.

November. New Zealand spring, apparently, and it was still freezing; as cold as a Scottish winter and windier than the top of Ben Nevis.

A diminutive girl had appeared in the doorway. Her face was almost covered by earmuffs and a bright red woolly hat with huge pompom, plus a matching scarf pulled up over her mouth. All Cal could see was her eyes. A dark penetrating brown that showed her to be at once apprehensive and excited. A common rookie air ambulance reaction. She pulled down her scarf and grinned. 'Hi, I'm Abbie. Staff nurse in ED. I was told to hitch a ride, see what you do out in the wild.'

'Er...hello.' Cal shifted over in the tiny space, glancing over at his companion, Shane, who was leading this shift.

Shane nodded back and smiled at the girl; clearly he knew her and liked her.

'Where should I sit?' Her eyes danced around

the cabin, her hands moving as she spoke, a vibrancy he hadn't seen before in anyone.

Shane lumbered up into the chopper, wheezing as he sat down. Poor bugger was just at the back end of the flu and letting everyone know about it. 'Shift over, Callum, make some room for our guest.'

It was none of Cal's business, but there was barely enough room in here as it was. Plus they'd have to fit the patient on the gurney and work on him if necessary. 'Going to be cosy.'

'It won't be for long. We can see Ben Lomond from here.' Abbie shuffled in next to him and buckled her belt. 'So, be gentle with me, eh?'

He looked at those dancing eyes and couldn't help smiling at her. 'First time?'

'First medivac. Not first time in a chopper. Don't you know, it's the only way to travel in Queenstown?' She bit her lip and explained, 'There's a lot of heli-sport here; heli-skiing, heli-hiking, that kind of thing.'

With a lurch they ascended. Helicopters didn't usually lurch. 'It's blowy, that's for sure.'

'Coming off the Remarkables. Along with snow, I reckon. There's a southern blast coming up from Antarctica.' She nodded and looked away, gripping her hands together. From this angle he could see the fine shape of her jawline and some tiny wrinkles by her eyes. Not as young as he'd first thought, then. Hair sticking out at all angles from under her hat. Long eyelashes. Geez, it was real cosy in here if he was paying attention to her eyelashes.

Kind of cute, too.

He gave himself a mental telling-off. He had no business thinking any woman was cute. Not when he had responsibilities elsewhere.

Still, a bit of window-shopping never harmed anyone...

'Great view, isn't it? I wouldn't live anywhere else on earth.' Having raised her voice a notch above the chopper blades' racket, Abbie pointed to the town below them. The deep blue lake stretched out as far as he could see, fringed on one side by the bustling centre of Queenstown. A string of gondolas swung directly beneath them, slowly scaling one of the mountains that framed the town. A zigzag luge was hundreds of feet below, where kids and adults alike risked life and limb—and had a lot of fun in the process— racing on go-karts down curved tracks to the valley. The girl grinned. 'You're not from here, right? Have you been on the luge yet?'

'Nah. But I've scooped a kid up from it and taken him to ED. Nasty grazes and a fractured elbow.'

'Makes you wary, then, does it? The adrenalin capital of the world?' Her eyes danced again.

If only she knew. Adrenalin was his best friend, and his worst enemy. Before he could answer, the earth started to come up to meet them and the pilot was saying something about a body at two o'clock. Cal scanned the snow, the steep ridge, the jutting rocks and thought he saw something that looked out of place. A flash of blue. Then, yes... 'He's over there. I can see him.'

'Yes. Yes. Watch out, it's going to be slippery,' the pilot shouted back, his words barely audible under the chug, chug, chug of the helicopter rotor blades. He'd made a spectacular landing on the only flat bit of mountainside—it took some skill to do that. 'Got your crampons?'

'Och, yes. I'll be fine, no worries.' If there was one thing Callum Baird knew it was snow. Every kind. The wet, seeping-through-your-clothes kind. The fluffy make-a-decent-snow-ball kind. And this, the melted and frozen again ice that meant getting a foot grip was challenging. Especially in the sixty-knot winds and poor visibility at the top of Ben Lomond. That last kind of snow was why he was here in the first place. To learn how to make amends, to try to fix things that probably couldn't be fixed, but to make things better, at least.

He hoped.

Funny, how he'd travelled halfway around the world and found himself on the top of a moun-

tain bearing the same damned name as the place
he'd left. Almost as beautiful, too. If the clouds
disappeared, and with a bit of spring sunshine
it'd be stunning…but he wasn't here to admire
the view.

Bracing against the wind, he jumped from
the helicopter then turned and grabbed his paramedic backpack. The crampons slipped on as
easily as the memories. He shook the latter off.
He was used to doing that. Some days they did
as they were told and slunk away, and he managed to get through twenty-four hours before he
was drawn back to that fateful night of cold and
wet and ice. Other days they hung around him,
a sopping, freezing bone-deep helplessness he
couldn't shake. 'From what I could see, our guy's
up there, to the right—it's fairly rocky, so we'll
have to do a bit of scrambling. He told Dispatch
he'd heard a snap, so we'd best take the scoop
with us, too. Hope you enjoy a bit of ice-skating?'

'Preferably on the flat.' Abbie assessed the
terrain, shook her head, then passed the scoop
down. 'I'm not sure I'd manage a triple Salchow
on this hill.'

'I'm not sure I'd manage a triple Salchow,
full stop.' So, she had a sense of humour. That
worked. Especially in conditions like this.

Due to the deteriorating weather, it had been
touch and go whether to bring the chopper up

here at all, but a man's life hung, literally, on the edge, so they'd made a call. A good one, as it turned out. The ride had been bumpy, but the wind seemed to be dying down, for now. Which meant hypothermia would be less of an issue for all of them. Two months living in New Zealand and the only thing he could predict about the weather was that it was unpredictable.

'You got crampons?'

'Doesn't every woman carry a pair in her handbag?' He watched as she delved into her backpack and pulled out a pair of ice shoes, which she fastened like a pro. 'Ready.'

Although giving him a reassuring smile, she looked frozen through. A tiny waif, with huge eyes and that mess of dark hair that was tumbling from clips in every direction. The huge hi-vis jacket swamped her, and she looked out of her depth on every level.

But determination shone in her eyes.

'Right. Let's get to it.' It was hard going— one step forward, steadying your grip. Another step. The snow had frozen to sheer ice in some places. In others, tufts of grass poked through. The wind pressed them back, the ice halted their steps, so they made it to their patient as quickly as humanly possible.

He was a crumpled heap in bright blue and black walking gear. Alone. Like many walkers here. Starting out on a pleasant day trip, but at least he seemed suitably dressed for the occasion, unlike some Cal came across. Still, even full walking gear didn't always prevent disaster from striking. You could be perfectly prepared for a night stranded on the mountain, but not for unexpected and complicated fractures, blizzards, nowhere to hide from the biting wind. Frostbite.

A brother lifeless in your arms and there is nothing, nothing you can do but pray. As they neared, Cal did a primary survey. Breathing. Bleeding from his forehead. Bluish lips. Thank God for cell-phone reception, or who knew when he'd have been found. Phoning for help had saved his life.

That was, if they could get him down quickly enough.

The wind might have died a little, but it was still fresh as all hell up here and their guy was shaking. Cold and shock, or worse. Cal remembered to keep his words slow. Enough people had told him they didn't understand his Scottish accent already. 'Hello, there. I'm Cal, your knight in shining hi-vis.'

Abbie rolled her eyes. 'And I'm Abbie. That guy down there is Shane, and we're going to help get you off the mountain. Now, can you tell us what happened?'

So, she was all about the process. Okay.

'I'm… Marty… I think I've…' Dazed and shivering, the patient tried to sit up.

'Whoa. Hold still, mate. Tell me what happened.' Secondary survey was underway. There was blood on the ground. Which meant consideration had to be made for internal bleeding too. *Blood on the floor and five more. Consider thoracic, intra-abdominal, retroperineal, pelvic, long bones.*

'Slipped. Fell down from the ridge. Hit my head, I think, on a rock. Chest… Leg snapped…' He reached a hand to his right fibula and grimaced. *Long bones.*

Plus, a head injury—couldn't rule out neck damage too. 'So, first things first, we need to put a neck brace on to protect that neck. Steady as you go. Hold still. Stay still, mate.' Cal slipped the neck brace into place, watching as Marty clenched his fists to counter the pain. Then bent his undamaged knee. At least he could move all his limbs. Good sign.

Cal had a closer look at the forehead wound. 'Looks pretty deep, needs a few stitches. Luckily, they're very good at sewing down at Queenstown General.' He taped a dressing over the wound, noting other minor cuts and grazes that would need attention, when they had more time, and in the warmth of a hospital ward.

Cal felt Marty's radial pulse. Nothing. Carotid

showed a rapid, thready heartbeat. 'Guessing the systolic pressure is lower than ninety. No radial pulse. I'll do a quick check. Needs some fluids.' Needed surgery, actually. Fluids and stabilisation were the best they could do, especially up here on the steep arc of a mountainside with thick black clouds coming in from the west. Cal's heart rate sped up a little.

Great. A suspected life-threatening injury and the mother of all storms.

Luckily, fighting the odds was what he was good at.

Shane finally made it up the mountain. Breathless and wheezing, he probably shouldn't have been up here at all. He should have said his chest wasn't up to it. But Cal kept that thought to himself.

The two-way radio crackled. It was Brian, the pilot. 'Weather coming in fast. We need to get off this mountain and quick. Over.'

'Things turn to custard pretty quick round here.' One minute it was sunny, the next it was a white-out. But they had to make Marty safe before they left. 'Okay. Let's have a look at your leg. I'm going to have to cut your salopettes. Okay? Damned shame, because it's good kit.'

Keeping the patient talking and conscious gave them a better chance, so Cal went with his usual patter. He nodded at Shane, who was assessing the obviously broken leg. The bone had cut through the skin. Needed a splint at least to stabilise it. Needed surgery.

Needed to get off the mountain, and fast.

Again, Marty pushed to sit up. 'I can't breathe… I can't…'

Cal shot a look at Abbie, who'd turned her attention to Marty's chest. Could be one of a dozen things. He prayed there wasn't any surgical emphysema. Dodgy lungs in thin air at the top of a mountain were a nasty prospect. 'I'm going to put a line in your left arm, mate. Give you some fluids to keep you hydrated and something to make you more comfortable.'

'Left lung clear, but can't hear much in the right base. You want to check?'

'Yep. Let me have a go. To check.' Not wanting to disbelieve her or undermine her, he listened as carefully as he could to the beat-up chest. Suspected right pneumothorax. Great. The odds were starting to turn against them. It was freezing up here; his hands were starting to ache with the cold.

'Oxygen in situ. Pain relief administered.'

'Leg splint inflated and in situ.' The distant clouds had become very real, thick and dark and heavy. Flakes started to spot their coats, Marty's hair.

'Pass me a survival blanket, will you? Right.

Thanks. Now, we've got to get you onto this scoop.'

The radio crackled. 'Cal, come in. You have two minutes. Over.'

'Just getting Marty on the scoop. Over.'

Cal positioned the scoop alongside their patient and somehow they managed to shift him over, keeping his neck as still as possible.

'Let's go. You all okay?' Shane took the lead, carrying the scoop at the feet end. Cal was at the head and Abbie walked at the side, carrying equipment and making sure Marty was stable and as comfortable as possible. It was like a game of slip 'n' slide getting them all down the hill.

'You fancy some tobogganing, Marty?' It was only half a joke. Apart from a few rocks it was a vertical skating rink.

They started to inch gingerly down. The sun had slid behind a cloud and the wind whipped round them, biting through their clothes. They made it a few metres then suddenly the scoop lurched sideways and forwards. Next thing Cal knew, Shane was yelling and tumbling head first over rocks and ice.

Down. Down. Down.

CHAPTER TWO

'SHANE! SHANE!'

The boss had come to a halt a hundred metres or so down the hill, splayed against the rear of the helicopter. He wasn't moving.

Cal reassessed, looking from Shane to Marty and then back down the slope again, allowing himself the briefest moment for his heart to thump hard and fast against his chest wall. Damn. *Damn.* Then he closed off all emotion.

Panic didn't help. Helplessness didn't help. Just action. He'd learnt his lesson the hard way. Had been learning for two long years.

Two patients now. One scoop and a fledgling helper.

Their patient took priority. Getting him down the hill now was going to be a challenge.

Somehow Callum had managed to keep a firm grip on Marty's scoop. 'You okay, mate?'

'Holding on,' he groaned. 'Just about.'

The scoop listed at a sharp forty-five-degree

angle, from where Cal had maintained his hold and height, to where Abbie had been twisted by the sudden lurch sideways and pushed to the floor. She was just about managing to hold the scoop aloft with her arms outstretched underneath Marty, bearing his weight in a desperate attempt to keep their patient still and secure. There was an ooze of blood on her head. 'Abbie? You okay?'

She grimaced, her body contorting in an effort to hold up the scoop and the man, who must have weighed three times what she did. 'I'm fine. It's okay.'

'You're bleeding.'

'It's nothing. I caught my head on a rock as I fell. It's just a scratch.' She shook her head, trying hard to pretend she was okay, but he could see right through it. 'You should see the other guy.'

'Sadly, I can see him.' The boss looked knocked out and flat. Marty was groaning in agony in the tipped-up scoop. And Abbie had a cut head.

It looked worse than just a scratch, but he had to believe her because he just couldn't do this alone. She seemed orientated and fine. Feisty, actually. He'd have a closer look once they were on safe terrain and out of danger. 'Right then.

I'm going to lower him down so we can right the scoop, then we can wait for Brian to come help.'

'He'd be better staying down there, don't you think? To see if Shane's okay?'

'I'll talk to him.' Cal shouted towards the chopper but couldn't make himself heard. He flicked on the two-way. 'Hey. Did you see Shane? He took a bad fall, he's at the rear. Roger.'

'I'm on my way. How are you going to manage with the scoop? Slide it down?'

'Not sure yet. Over.' There were too many rocks sticking out of the ground to make sliding a feasible option.

'She's a little thing. Roger.'

'We'll be fine.' It was Abbie, glowering. She had the affronted air of someone who would not be underestimated. He knew that trait well. Too well. Someone who insisted on overstretching... and then paying the consequences. She'd lowered her side of the scoop now and was brushing the snow and ice from her clothes. As she bent to the left she winced. 'Just give me a couple of seconds.'

They barely had one. The weather was closing in. This was all falling apart, but he needed to stay in control. 'Are you hurt? Is it something more than your head? Did the scoop hit you?'

'Just winded me.' She shook her head again

but he could see the way she flinched as she turned. 'Let's do this.'

'I can call back-up. You won't be able to manage.'

'Says who? I could be a champion weightlifter for all you know. I could have won the Queenstown Primary arm wrestling competition in 1997.' She flexed her arms, but all he could see was the huge coat covering her from neck to knee. With the head wound and her wayward hair and the enormous coat she looked like a bag lady rather than the professional she was proving to be. 'What do you think, Marty? Am I stronger than I look?'

'I hope so,' Marty groaned. 'Yes.'

She gave Cal an I-told-you-so grin that made her eyes light up and his stomach feel strange, then she shuffled to the end of the scoop and bent in readiness to pick it up. 'So, let's do this. What choice do we have?'

'We could wait for back up. Or Brian.' But even with the space blanket, Marty was shaking with cold; they had to get this done and quick.

'He's with Shane and it looks like he needs help too.' Too true. Brian was trying to lift Shane up, but the senior paramedic kept buckling forward. She glanced at the swirls of snow falling around them. 'There isn't a choice. We have to do this or we'll all freeze to death.' Without any further chance at a conversation she bent at the end of the scoop and shouted, 'Ready? On my call. One. Two. Three.'

They were badly matched size-wise, but if he kept his arms straight and stooped down low they were just about able to maintain a satisfactory balance. But it was slow going. He could see every muscle in her hands tighten and strain as she bore the weight of the hiker.

She doesn't have gloves on.

Somewhere along the way she'd taken them off—to work the IV and draw up drugs, probably. And hadn't had the chance to put them back on. Her fingers were white—with strain? With cold?

That was all he needed. Frostbite.

Frostbite. The enemy of the winter hiker. Could do untold damage from the inside out.

The dread swamped him along with the memories. He wasn't going to let that happen. They were getting off this mountain without any further incident. Stooping low, he gripped harder and tried to take more of the weight. It was impossible without upending the whole thing. Regardless of how strong she thought she was, she was starting to tire—steps becoming slower as she navigated the rocks. She needed to rest without losing face, he got that. 'Stop. Stop, Abbie. I need a minute.'

'Oh. Okay.' Very gently she lowered her end of the scoop then straightened up, twisting slowly left and right to ease out her muscles. Her hands were still in crooked fists and even from this distance he could see red marks on her palms. More blood?

'Brian! Brian, come here and take over.' They were about fifty metres from the chopper. Shane was sitting slumped against the landing gear holding his shoulder. 'You go down and take over from Brian and he can come and help me with this.'

'I can do this.'

He kept his voice level despite his growing frustration. 'And I'm telling you not to. Your hands are cut and cold and there's no need for you to lift anything if we can get Brian to do it. I need you down there to sort out Shane. He's not looking happy. Brian's just a pilot—he can't assess anything. I need your nursing skills and his muscle.'

'Okay. I'm gone.'

He was impressed with the agility and speed with which she made it to Shane, crossing paths with Brian and stopping for the briefest of handovers.

He watched as she tripped lightly over the rocks, that jacket swamping her tiny frame. She had guts, that was for sure. In another life he might have…

No, he wouldn't.

No point in wishing. He didn't have space for a relationship; and definitely not with someone a million miles away from his home. That would never work. No point starting something.

He pressed forwards, forcing all his attention to the here and now, not the murky past or his short-circuited future.

Finally, they were all settled into the chopper. Two patients. One more than they'd bargained for.

Brian gunned the engine. 'It's going to be a bit bumpy, but we'll be back in no time.'

She looked a little green as they rose into the air and shunted sharply east as a rogue gust caught them. For one second she looked terrified, then she regained her composure and started to chat to Shane, keeping him orientated to time and place. Her voice was like music cutting through the grim roar of the engine and the beeping of the portable ECG machine that monitored Marty's heart trace.

She was laughing, but it was gentle and lyrical. 'So, Shane, your crampon front-ended and you did a spectacular cartwheel down the mountain. If you want to train for the gymnastic world championships you could do with finding a more level place to do it.'

'Er…what's…happening? Did we have a patient?'

There was a flicker of a frown, then she recovered. 'Yes. He's just here, next to you. Marty's had some ketamine so he's doing okay. No. No, stay where you are, love. We need you to keep as still as you can.' All the while she talked, her eyes roved over first one patient then the other, assessing, monitoring, smiling.

Dancing. Moving. Smiling.

There was just something about her that was mesmerising.

Cal shook himself and focused on Marty's observations. Mesmerising or not, he had promises to fulfil. Three months, he'd been given. Three months to train with the most highly skilled search and rescue team in the world and then he'd be back in Scotland to resume his duties and try to make amends for the mistake that had cost his brother his future.

By the time they reached the ED it was almost the end of Abbie's shift. Her head was thumping a little but the bleeding had stopped. And, okay, she'd lied. The scoop had been so heavy, her hands were cut and sore, but none of that mattered until Marty and Shane were sorted out.

Having already taken Shane through to her waiting colleagues, she now helped wheel Marty's gurney into Resus and handed over to the ED staff. Into safe hands.

Theoretically, from this side of the process, she was done, but she hung around, feeling a little sidelined and a lot out of sorts. Actually, she was in pain and a little shocked at how things had progressed in those wintry conditions and how close they'd come to disaster. Cal was standing next to her. He looked up from his notes, those bright eyes catching her by surprise. He was a big man. Tall. Broad. Calm. He glanced at her forehead. 'You need to get that cut sorted out. I'll ask someone to take a look.'

'I'll sort it. Thanks. They're all too busy with Marty and Shane and a load of other things.' She swiped the back of her hand across her forehead. 'It's all dried up. I'll do it later.'

'Or, I'll do it for you, now.' He pointed to an empty cubicle. 'Grab a seat.'

'But I want to stay and work on Marty.'

'Tough luck. Not your job right now.' A straight talker, then. As he spoke Cal wheeled round and opened a few drawers, finding some gauze and saline.

'Actually, it *is* my job. I can't just abandon my shift.'

'I'm not asking you to, but you're my responsibility right now—you hurt yourself on my watch.'

'It was hardly your fault; we did what we had to do. This is just a bit of fallout. I'll live.'

'But I'm duty bound to fix you up. Plus, I can't let you tend to any patients looking like that—you'll scare them off.' His eyes glinted with laughter and she couldn't help joining in. Next thing she knew he was moving her to a seat and pressing the gauze onto her forehead. He'd been firm but fair up the mountain, having been thrust in charge of three—no, four, including the pilot—lives. Clearly, he was the kind of guy who took responsibility seriously. He hadn't been flustered or snappy, he'd just calmly told them all what they needed to do. A leader by example. And here he was doing it again.

He was also incredibly close. She couldn't remember being this close to a man who wasn't her patient for a long time. A long, long time. He was still being all calm and in control—if not a little bossy. And that made her nervous inside.

And…and he had the most amazing scent. A fresh air kind of smell. Something she wanted to inhale.

Stop it. She could feel her cheeks starting to burn. 'Look, give me the saline, I'll just wipe it—'

'No.' His voice was level and steady and she

got the feeling he wasn't going to cave in to her refusal. 'Sit down and let me clean this up. This is going to sting.'

'Are you, by chance, an older brother?'

'Yeah. How did you guess?' There was a grim smile at that comment, his eyes dulling a little.

'Oh, you know, the take-no-crap bossiness. I bet your sibs love you.'

'As it happens, he does. One brother. Younger, by two and a half years. He hates me and loves me in equal measure.' There was a pause where Callum seemed to retreat into his own thoughts, his eyes clouded with pain that seemed to come from nowhere, but permeated his body. 'No, actually he just hates me.'

'Boys will be boys, I guess.'

'Something like that.' Cal took her hand and started to open the fist she'd made to try to keep the blood circulating, because to straighten out the broken skin hurt. A lot. Instead of thinking about the pain she focused on what he was saying, and what he was leaving out. It wasn't *something like that* at all; she could tell. His manner had changed. He'd shut down a little at the mention of his brother. Or maybe she was just imagining it. She couldn't fathom why she'd even noticed, and why his reticence intrigued her. He touched her fingertips lightly and they began to tingle. 'Let me see your hands properly.'

'Oh. Ouch. Remember when I said, *be gentle with me*? Yeah...that.'

Compared to the rounds and rounds of IVF she'd been through, the head wound was a walk in the park. Her hands, though—they were still frozen and cut and she just knew if he saw them he'd flip out. Because he was that kind of guy. The protective sort. The thought of which made her stomach constrict. She'd had one of them. A wonderful, amazing protective man who'd held her heart so tightly she couldn't imagine giving it to anyone else. She didn't need to, or want to. So she had no right to be thinking about Cal's eyes or manner, let alone getting carried away with smelling his scent. 'My fingers are starting to thaw out...you know that weird buzzy feeling?'

'Aha. Only too well.' He peeled her fingers open and sucked in a breath at the sight of her raw, bleeding skin. 'You shouldn't have carried such a heavy weight, or you should have put your gloves on to protect yourself.'

'Should have, would have, could have. There wasn't time, remember? None of it is important, anyway. Marty's safe and Shane's being looked at. That's all that matters. Right?'

But he'd zoned out, looking at her wedding ring. He was all matter-of-fact when he spoke. 'Yes, well, all fixed up now. How are your feet?'

She stamped her boots and wiggled her toes.

Luckily she'd put extra-thick socks on today. 'Feet are just fine. Thank you. I'm good to go.'

'And I'm in charge of this shift now that Shane's indisposed, so finally, just one last thing: you need to get a hot drink inside of you and something to eat before you do anything else. We need to debrief before the next call if possible. Definitely time for a break. Paramedic's orders.'

'I'm fine.'

'You usually have blue fingers?'

Looking first at him then back at her hands, she realised there was no point in arguing. He was, in fact, right. She was still freezing and hadn't had a drink in hours. She'd be no use to anyone like this. But she wasn't letting him know that. And, if she was absolutely honest, she wanted a couple more minutes with him— it had been a strange day and debriefing was a great idea. With a theatrical sigh she rolled her eyes. 'Definitely an older sib.'

Could have done a lot better. Cal looked at the inexpertly applied gauze on her forehead and inwardly cringed. It looked as if it had been stuck on by a kindergarten kid.

It was because he was cold; that was what he was telling himself, anyway. And not because there was anything going on here—like attraction. Given he was heading out of town soon, attraction was a spectacularly bad idea.

Because of her wound, her bobble hat was pushed back, so more tufts of dark, coffee-coloured hair stuck out around her face. She looked as if she'd been...well, as if she'd been on the top of a mountain in a hurricane. It was lucky she'd been there as an extra pair of hands—albeit damaged in the process. She'd coped well, but his heart had only just about started to beat normally again. The SARS training had given him confidence he'd have been able to deal with anything up there, but he hadn't wanted to test it.

He paid for the flat white and handed it to her, wondering what this urge to chat with her was all about. He didn't usually buy Shane a cuppa and *debrief.* Yeah, right...great chat-up line; that'd have them all laughing back at base. The closest they ever got to debriefing for real was a quick chat on the ride to the next emergency, scoffing a lukewarm pie and bad coffee from the petrol station.

They steered through the busy cafeteria and found an empty table. Once they'd settled in, he broke up his bar of chocolate and offered some to her. 'Eat; you'll be better with something inside you to bring up the blood sugar.'

She blinked. 'You really *do* do a lot of bossing around.'

'Sorry. Bad habit of mine. You're not the first person to tell me that. It's a kind of misguided attempt to look after you.' Instead of analysing his faults—he was aware he had a few, because Finn made it his personal mission to highlight every single one of his brother's shortcomings—he went for a change of subject. 'So, you had a baptism of fire up there. You handled it all very well, though. Not bad for a newbie.'

Underneath the huge jacket, she bristled. 'I've been a nurse for a long time. I'm just new at ED, that's all. Well, I've been here a few months. But it's a big learning curve, right?'

'When you're out in the field, yes. You don't know what's going to be thrown at you.'

She took a sip and seemed to settle a little. 'I haven't seen you here before, though.'

'Different shifts probably, and I've been out at Wanaka a lot and with the SARS team. I've only been in New Zealand a couple of months all up.' Which reminded him that spending what little time he had left talking to women he could never see again was pretty pointless. Although very nice. Actually, more than nice.

'And you're from… Scotland? Is that right?'

'Aye.' The familiar tug of responsibility tight-ened in his gut. He needed to get back there. Wasting another month here felt as if he were killing time. Time he could be using to sort Finn out. But, he'd promised to get as much training as he could and he didn't want to go back unqualified, or to seem ungrateful to everyone who'd pushed him to come here in the first place. 'Another month then I'm gone.'

She nodded before blowing on the steaming drink. 'Of course you are.'

An odd reply. 'What does that mean?'

'The majority of people working in Queenstown are just passing through, so I'm not surprised you'll be going, too. Where next? Aussie? Asia? The big OE we call it. Overseas Experience. A gap year?'

'At twenty-nine, I'm a bit too old for a gap year. Honestly. No travelling, I'm going straight back home.'

She looked surprised. 'So you did all your travelling before coming here?'

'No. I'm not travelling. I came to do specialist search and rescue training. For my job. I have...' And here was the thing—he was suddenly torn. The minute he'd been needed he'd pledged to spend the rest of his life looking after his brother. This trip had been the first glimpse of how life could have been, but nothing was going to stop him going back. Finn needed him. 'I have responsibilities back home.'

Was he dreaming or did she look at his hand? For a wedding ring? Laughable. He had enough to do without taking on someone else. 'Well, they'll be glad to have you back, I'm sure.'

He smiled. She didn't know the half of it. 'I doubt it. But I'm going anyway. What about you? Obviously a Kiwi…?'

She smiled right back. Looked straight into his eyes, and he got a warm sensation swimming through him. 'I've lived in Queenstown my whole life. Been out of the country a few times for holidays, but always came straight back here. It's where my family is.'

'You're not one of those New Zealanders who has the travel bug, then?'

'No. I need to stay here.' At his raised eyebrows she continued, 'Responsibilities too.'

'Oh—?' But of course. He'd noticed the wedding ring on her finger before. That was okay. He could do platonic. Yeah, platonic was good. Maybe then he wouldn't be so mesmerised by her.

Odd, but she quickly drained her coffee and looked at something behind him, her eyes darting and dancing, kind of nervous, kind of sad. 'Oh-oh, caught in the act. My boss is heading over. I've got to go.'

'Hey, Cal.' It was Steph from ED. 'Abbie, sorry to disturb you. I heard you did well today. Awesome job.'

'Thanks. It was…' She caught Cal's eye and

smiled. A shared day, shared joke, shared rescue. There was always a bit of a connection after that. 'Interesting.'

'You left this on the desk, I thought you might want to keep it safe.' Steph handed her an ultrasound picture. He was no expert, but it looked like an antenatal one. Yep—even from here he could make out the shape of a baby.

She's having a baby.

'Thank you. Yes. Oh, goodness. My scan.' Abbie's eyes were filled with pride that gave Cal a strange jolt in his gut.

Steph ambled on chatting as white noise filled his head. 'Thought of any names yet? Did you ask about the gender?'

'No. We're going to wait. It's exciting, though. I can't believe that by Christmas there's going to be a baby here.

She's having a baby.

A bairn.

His overprotective gene fired into action. Finn would have laughed as usual and told him to back right off, but Cal couldn't help it. This was serious. He waited until Steph had gone, then, 'You didn't tell me you were pregnant. Up there. In the snow. You fell over. I let you carry a heavy weight. Why did you let me think you were okay?'

'I am okay. I'm fine, actually. Honestly.' She

didn't even look a little contrite. What a dangerous game she'd been playing. And he shouldn't
care, not at all, but for some reason he was fir-
ing on all protection cylinders today.

Maybe he was missing Finn. Missing the opportunity to care and be useful. *To fuss and
smother,* as Finn would say.

'You carried that scoop, which would have put
a strain on your whole body, and you hurt your
side. You were wincing and it's obvious you still
have some pain.'

She shook her head. 'It's nothing, just a pulled
muscle. Really, I'm fine.'

Yeah, he'd heard that before. When his brother
wanted him to believe everything was okay. It
hadn't been. It had been far from okay. He wasn't
buying it. He stood up. 'I want you to get looked
over. I'm not listening to any excuses…you need
to be checked out. An ultrasound or something.'

'Who are you? My mother?' But she was smiling. Smiling and moving and dancing. *Really?*
He knew she was committed to someone else.
Married, for God's sake. He needed his head
looking at.

'I'm just concerned, Abbie. You could have
hurt—'

'My baby?' she cut in, laughing. 'Don't worry,
Callum. My baby is…' she nodded towards a

pregnant woman walking towards them '...over there.'

What?

He did the maths, joined the dots, put all the jigsaw pieces into place.

Ah.

How could he have got it so wrong? His gay radar wasn't working today. 'Oh. I see. Your partner's having your baby...your *wife*?'

She rubbed her fingers over her wedding ring and laughed. 'You really have got it *so* wrong, I can't begin to tell you. But I've got to go. I've a very important coffee date. Thanks for warming me up.' Then she paused, blushed, her eyes meeting his in a very heterosexual kind of way. He could see something there that was just for him—a softening, a little bit of playfulness, a very timid flirt. Or was there? Was he going mad? There was definitely a connection here he just did not understand. She shook her head, dragging her gaze from his. 'I mean... Well... thanks.'

CHAPTER THREE

COULD I HAVE been any more tongue-tied? Eurgh.

It had been three days since she'd had that strange afternoon with Callum, and every time Abbie thought about it she cringed and blushed. Even when she was on her own.

She should have been upfront with him but she'd been cold and tired and excited about the baby and…flustered.

The man made her flustered.

Which was why she'd decided to go for a run—to purge those feelings, all of them, from her system. God knew she had enough on her mind without trying to work out why a man was making her lost for words.

It was the shoulder season, but in Queenstown that still meant a lot of visitors filling the buzzing town centre. A coach pulled up lakeside, spilling passengers for the *TSS Earnslaw* steamship cruise. The tourists, all rugged up in matching waterproofs and chattering excitedly, weren't looking where they were going, so Abbie had to zigzag round them.

'On your left,' she called out, hoping they'd move for a slightly uncoordinated runner. She could hardly blame them for being excited, though; the sun was out in the cloudless sky and it finally felt like spring. Although, that could easily change.

Not accidentally photo-bombing or running into the crowds was difficult and Abbie craved some quiet thinking time, so she headed along past the gardens and out onto the lakeside bike trail.

For a few kilometres or so she shared the track with cyclists and other runners, but eventually she was on her own, breathing hard and trying not to trip over wayward tree roots and little rocks sticking up at irregular intervals as she navigated through bush.

Eventually, she found her rhythm, blissfully unaware of anything else but her feet hitting the ground, the rustle of the trees, birdsong. Then, the bit she liked best of all—the trail opening up from bush to a wide track, and the view of the lake, which, as always, took her breath away.

Up ahead there was a figure sitting on a bench. Great place to smell the roses, if you had the time. Sitting didn't do a lot for Abbie. Ever since Michael died she'd been running, exer-

cising, anything to get rid of the excess energy
that seemed to spiral through her. Anxiety didn't
hang around when her lungs were pumping nine-
teen to the dozen. Endorphins worked too. Happy
hormones—she needed them. Especially now.

As she closed in she heard talking. Bench Man
was on the phone.

'What d'ya mean, you've been out on *The
Cairnwell*? For God's sake, Finn, will you lis-
ten to me—? I don't care if it's the easiest one.
You will not go there again, d'you hear me?'

Cal?

Just when she'd thought her heart couldn't beat
any faster it sped up even more. She slowed right
down. Even though she was feeling guilty about
playing him along, now clearly wasn't the right
time to fix things. He had no clue he was being
watched and she felt a worm of discomfort twist
in her tummy. If she entered the clearing he'd
see her; right now she was camouflaged by the
trees. But it felt as if she was eavesdropping on
a very private conversation.

'Aye, well, I'm sorry about that. Did you take
your meds?'

He was facing away from her, his back rigid.
Shoulder muscles she hadn't seen the other day
due to his hi-vis were well defined…taut. He was
wearing sports gear too—a loose-fitting singlet
and shorts. Running?

'Why the hell not? Well, you'd better start. Things are going to change when I get back. And how.'

He flicked his phone into his pocket and stood, staring out across the water, every sinew tense.

Now she didn't know what to do. Run? Walk? Say something? Nothing? Turn around and go home? Was he going to come towards her, or race off in front?

But he bent for a moment, lifting his foot onto the bench and checking his laces. If he turned his head even the tiniest fraction he'd see her. She'd be caught watching him. So not a good idea.

He looked the other way, along the path.

Now was her chance. She ducked out from behind the trees and sped along the trail.

'Race you!' she called as she overtook him.

What the hell...? Where had that come from? Her mouth had a mind of its own—and it was a little out of control. Damned endorphins must have kicked in early today.

'What?' He jumped at her voice, did a double take. 'Do I know—?'

'Come on.' Then, for some reason she didn't understand, she turned around and jogged backwards, slowly, until he caught her up. She threw him a gauntlet. 'Going to the bridge? I can give you a head start if you need it?'

'Abbie?' His gaze skimmed her body—for the

first time ever she felt unbearably underdressed in full-length running tights and a razor-back top. And suddenly very hot. But then, she had been running. His amazing eyes met hers and he grinned. Not the faintest hint of breathlessness anywhere in him. 'Well, wow. Unexpected. Hello.'

'I can hang back, let you go ahead if you need to.'

The irritation she'd seen in him while on the phone disappeared and he laughed. 'Not necessary. Challenge accepted.'

'To the bridge?'

'Seriously?'

There was a moment when she almost felt sorry for him. 'You underestimate me at your peril.'

Then there was no more talking.

They were evenly matched…at least, at first. She met him stride for stride and only when the path narrowed did she fall behind a little. All the better to get another view of those amazing muscles. He was either a climber, or he worked out. No one had that kind of upper-body strength just by lifting gurneys.

But when he sensed her close behind him he pulled sharply to the right to let her join him again. The bridge was in sight. She let him think she was going to let the friendly camaraderie continue, then, with fifty metres to go, she sprinted out. Hard. Fast.

He got there at the same time. Laughing, reaching for the stone wall to tag. 'Well, you're fast, that's for sure.'

She decided not to tell him her reasons for running these days. Some things should be kept private. Besides, she could barely manage words. She hauled gulp after gulp of air as she bent over, hands on knees. 'Ran for…Otago. Back…in…the day. School…cross-country champion.'

'What? Like, last year?'

'Over ten years ago.' She pulled up, hands on hips. 'I know, I know, everyone always says I look young…but I'm as old as Methuselah really. Twenty-nine. Believe me… I've lived a little.'

'Ach, the wild child of Queenstown?'

Hardly. She'd been married at twenty-three. Felt ancient at twenty-five when she'd unexpectedly hit most of the ageing milestones far too soon—a married woman and then a widow. Sadly, the family bit had passed her by. 'Not quite. Let's just say, it's been an interesting ride.'

Without discussing where they were headed they started to walk back towards Queenstown centre. Yes, she could easily have run, but she didn't want to tire the poor thing out. 'And you? A wild child of…?'

'Duncraggen.' He tipped his head back and

laughed. 'The only thing that's wild up there is the weather. Oh, and the sheep.'

'Where's that? Dun…crabbing?'

'The very tip of Loch Lomond, a tiny wee village near Inverarnan. Not a lot about it, really.'

'So Queenstown must be the big scary metropolis, then?'

'I did live in Edinburgh for a while. And I have travelled a fair bit…in my youth.' He made a creaking sound. 'But now, young whippersnapper, I'm over the hill.'

'Oh, don't be too hard on yourself.' Where was this coming from? It felt natural to joke with him. 'You don't look a day over seventy.'

'Cheeky.' He threw her a sideways look and she could see laughter in his eyes. It was so nice to see that. A man who didn't take himself too seriously.

But then she remembered the untruth she'd let him believe. Not quite a lie, because he hadn't outright asked her, but not the truth either.

'Look, I've got a confession to make. I let you think that I'm…that I'm married to Emma.' If her cheeks could have got any redder they would have. As it was, she was puce from running and the cold wind on her face but having to put things straight was more than a little embarrassing. 'Thing is… It's, well…'

She'd got over talking about Michael's death

without crying. The grief didn't overwhelm her as it used to. She could go a few days without that lurching feeling in her stomach when she thought about him. But explaining it to Cal felt difficult, for some reason. Never mind the whole *someone else is cooking our baby* bit.

'It's what?' Cal stopped, his eyebrows knotting together as he looked at her. They'd come up to a quaint old café overlooking the lake and he pointed to it. 'Tell you what, let's have a coffee. Something stronger? You look like you need it and I have to confess, I'm all intrigued.'

Sit down and analyse everything? No, thanks. 'You know, I'm actually happy moving and talking.'

He was still smiling. 'Yes, I got that the first time I met you.'

'Really?' He'd noticed her? There was a little thrill in her stomach. A strange long-forgotten feeling, as if her body was remembering how it was supposed to work. She'd been on autopilot for so long—just breathing and surviving—this was new and different and not a little scary.

They began to amble along the path and, even though it felt strange, she had to admit it was actually quite nice to be in the company of a man for a change. Emma was her best friend and they talked about anything and everything, but this was…different. Interesting. She drew the line at *exciting*, because she wasn't going to allow herself to feel that, despite her tummy going all out with its little butterflies. 'Anyway, Emma said I was mean to let you think we were in a relationship, when nothing could be further from the truth. Em is my friend, that's all.'

He cleared his throat. 'I see. You're not married to her. You're not gay?'

'Not even a little bit. She really laughed at that bit, said I wasn't her type.'

Did she imagine it or did his breathing hitch a little? Did his pupils dilate ever so slightly? Probably not. 'Ah, so it's her baby…but you're great friends, so you refer to it as yours too? Am I any closer?'

'Not exactly. Maybe we should have had that coffee after all.' She sighed and took a few more breaths of perfectly cold refreshing air. Everyone at the hospital knew what had happened to her husband. All her family and friends had been so very supportive, so she didn't ever have to explain it to anyone new. Because there was never anyone new in her life. Until now.

But wait! Cal wasn't in her life. He was just another traveller passing through. Regardless, she did owe him an explanation. It wasn't as if he couldn't ask anyone at work—Shane even, when he was discharged—and they'd tell him anyway. It just felt better if she said it. 'Okay…

so, I'm wearing a ring because I was married to a wonderful man, but he got cancer and died before we could have any kids. So Emma's having one for us.'

She'd said it so fast she thought he might not have caught up with it all, but clearly he had, as it made him actually stop in his tracks. 'Whoa.'

'I know.' The thought of the baby made her smile. The thought of Michael made her sad. It was how it was: a see-sawing of emotion. Her life. It was so much easier talking about this as they moved along the track rather than face to face in the café, with all that intimate intensity and not being able to avoid the eye contact that brought with it.

But Cal was all amazing eyes and concern. 'You really have been through a lot. I don't even know where to begin here. There are so many questions—and I understand if you don't want to answer them. I don't even know if I should ask them.'

'It's okay.'

'I don't even know what to ask…your husband… So…how long ago…did he…?'

'Michael. His name was Michael. He died coming up to four years ago.'

He glanced down at the ring. 'I see.'

He didn't have to say another word. She'd spent so long wishing Michael were here, and she still did wish that. So much. She picked up the pace again. 'Yes, I still wear the ring. I'm still married in my heart, you see.'

'Aha. And the baby? This is where it gets confusing for a soft-headed man like myself.' He scratched his chin and frowned and she knew he was just playing her, but it was confusing, even for her, and she knew exactly what was going on.

'I can't, you know, have one. Have any. So Emma said she'd do it for me. Surrogacy. She's going to give me the baby when it comes.' *I hope.*

His eyes narrowed. 'You have concerns she might want to keep it?'

Had she actually said that out loud? 'No, not at all. It's just, I've been thinking long and hard about this recently, and I'm so very, very grateful to her. She's giving me my dream. We always wanted kids, you know? But when I look deep into my heart, I don't think I could do it. I don't think I could carry a baby and then give it to someone else.'

His voice was softer when he spoke. 'It's amazing what you'll do for someone you love.'

He was quiet for a few moments then—not a difficult kind of quiet, more a sad one. And yet, it wasn't a sad conversation or a sad prospect, not really. She was getting the one thing that she wanted. So, she presumed, he must have been sad about something else. 'I'm sorry, I didn't mean to bring it up…to make you feel awkward or anything.'

As if brushing off a memory, he shook his head. The smile was back, although a little less spectacular than before. 'Not awkward. Not at all. When's it due?'

'Twenty-third of December.' A Christmas baby. She hugged that delicious thought to herself.

But, like a mind-reader, he nodded. 'Just in time for Christmas.'

'I used to love Christmas. This is just going to make everything better again.'

'I hope so. Sounds perfect. If that's what you want.'

Clearly it wasn't what he wanted.

Why had she even told him all this? Why had she told him any of it? It wasn't like her to just blurt out her past history and her worries to a… stranger. He was a stranger. With a nice face. And amazing eyes. But he was still a stranger. A stranger who obviously had troubles of his own, had known difficult times.

'Anyway. That's me. Complicated doesn't begin to describe it. But… I don't know, I just felt like I owed you an explanation.'

'Abbie, you don't owe me anything. What you do is your business. I'm sure it'll all work out and you'll be very happy.'

'I hope so.'

'After what you've been through, you deserve some good times.' Without any warning, he sloped his arm around her shoulder and pulled her into a sideways hug. Just a squeeze, really, a friendly you'll-be-fine kind of thing, not anything meaningful. But her heart thumped at his touch. Her skin prickled. She inhaled his smell and thought, *Nice*. More than nice. There was that little butterfly stretching its wings in her stomach again. She pulled away.

They were still a little way from town, so she couldn't do what she naturally felt like doing, which was running. Running away from this feeling. From his hug. From this very nice man who was making her heart trip just a little too much. So she turned her attention onto him. All the better to put her own emotions and history back in their box. 'What about you? Family?'

'Just the brother. For the foreseeable future and beyond.'

When he'd spoken the other day about having to go back to Scotland for his responsibilities she'd presumed he'd meant family. A wife. Kids, maybe. And then she checked herself, because assumptions were what had made her feel uncomfortable when the staff had been talking about her. Just a brother seemed a strange reason to take himself halfway round the globe—clearly they had strong ties. 'Is that who you were talking to earlier?'

He rolled his eyes. 'You heard, eh? He's being a jerk. But then he thinks I'm being a jerk. So it's situation normal for the Baird brothers.'

'The bossy sibling strikes again?'

'Yeah. But the less said about that, the better. Let's not dwell on my baby brother. Don't want to ruin a perfectly nice day.' And there wasn't anywhere to go with that; he had that set-jaw look that she'd seen too many times on Michael to know he wasn't going to elucidate.

'Okay. So, no wife? Or husband?'

'No. Neither. And, I'm not having anyone's baby.' The light was back in his eyes now and he laughed, flattening his T-shirt over very flat-looking abs. 'This is just beer and good New Zealand *kai*.'

'Let's run it off, then!' And they were back to being silly and laughing and doing little spurts of sprints and star jumps, then a final race to the big red and white First World War memorial archway.

She got there first. Obviously. 'You're going to have to do better than that next time.'

Next time?

'Ach, well, I don't want to tell you this, but I did slow up just to let you think you'd won.'

'Too funny.' She flicked her hand across his

shoulder. He was a good guy. But a liar. 'You did not. I could see you really pushing all out.'

'Aye, well maybe. Or maybe not, you'll never actually know, will you? Besides, I have strength in other areas.' The way his mouth tipped up made her fixate on his lips. They were lovely. He had the best kind of smile.

She was still looking at his mouth as she spoke. 'Hmm...strengths? Sounds interesting?'

Flirting? Was she flirting?

'When's your next day off? I'll show you.'

'What? When? Me? No. I couldn't.'

His hands were on his hips now as he teased her. 'Scared? Don't want to be beaten, is that it?'

Was this a date? No, it wasn't a date. They both knew a date would be stupid. She didn't want a man...and definitely not a man who was leaving and who had something sad in his past that was dragging him back to places he didn't want to go. But he was going anyway.

She'd already had one man leave her. One perfect, irreplaceable husband. This was just... something to do with her day off. And a bet of sorts now, as well. She couldn't turn down a bet. 'Never. Tuesday. Day off.'

'Right. Meet you here at ten.' He tapped the stone archway. 'Prepare yourself for some fun.'

Fun? What the hell was that? She shouldn't be messing around with him. She had a whole heap of things to do to get ready for the baby. Her next day off should be spent shopping, cleaning, antenatal class tour of the maternity unit… 'I'll have to be done by two o'clock, though.'

'Right. See ya, then.' With a wink he turned and ran off around the edge of the lake, scattering the sleeping ducks and seagulls as he went, filling the sky with squawks and cries and feathers. His long limbs moved with surprising grace, his body clearly attuned to exercise.

There was so much adrenalin going through her she should have run too, but she hung back and watched him disappear into the milling crowds. A quick wave. That smile. And the butterflies began to dance in her stomach again.

But it was far easier to watch him run than to examine what was going on inside herself.

CHAPTER FOUR

'MAKE HER BREATHE. Make her breathe.'

The floppy toddler was thrust into his arms and Cal was on full alert. They were fighting the clock—hell, in this job they were always fighting the clock—but getting some adrenalin into this wee mite was the only thing that was going to fix her breathing.

With a history of allergies, she'd responded to the rogue peanut in her bestie's smuggled-in kindergarten snack like a pro. Many kids got flushed skin when they started to react to an allergen, but some went pale. Not pale enough to alert a carer necessarily, so warning signs weren't always noticed at first.

Ava was now ghostly pale and her face grossly swollen, so much so her eyes were barely visible. The allergic reaction was already in full flow. Tight wheezes came from her chest, otherwise she was eerily quiet as she stared up at him. The rest of the kindy kids had been ushered outside to play in the sunshine, their happy chatter the only noise breaking through that of the toddler's restricted breaths.

Geez, if ever he needed a distraction from the enigmatic Abbie, this was it. He'd not been able to get her out of his head for the last few days and every time he'd delivered a patient to the ED he'd found himself looking out for her. Their paths hadn't crossed since the run. Which was of no consequence right now.

'Hey, sweetie. Not feeling too good today?' It was always the little ones that got him the most. They were the ones that kept him awake at night, no matter how much he tried to put them out of his head. It was their faces he saw when he closed his eyes. The sweet damp baby perfume that lingered, along with the smell of fear from their parents. At least then it wasn't Finn's face and the heavy weight of panic tight in Cal's chest.

Having run in from the first responder car, he'd brought no gurney, so he lay Ava on a blanket on the well-worn carpet and started to draw up the age-suitable adrenalin. 'I'm going to give you a little injection, baby girl. That's going to help everything. Okay? Okay, Ava. Can someone gently hold her to stop wriggling? Great. Here we go.'

'Wait.' Just as he was about to administer the injection the teacher gave out a wail. She was equally pale and shaking as she held the tot's legs. 'Mum's not here. I can't... I can't give consent. Can I?'

'Lady, I'm giving consent.' This really wasn't the time for semantics. He had a duty of care and right now he was the only one able to save this kid's life. He raised his hand again and jabbed the needle into the little girl's thigh, watching as she screwed her face tightly. But not a whimper. Probably didn't have the energy to, she was so busy fighting her body's reaction, and failing. Just the roll of a lip, and what he could see of her eyes filled. He stroked back thick blonde curls, trying to keep emotion from rolling thick and fast into his chest, all the time assessing. Assessment beat emotion, every single time. Later, in the privacy of his own home, he'd go over his actions and his reactions. He'd allow the brief jolt of fear, then he'd remind himself he'd saved another life. The numbers were stacking up in his favour but it was the near misses he re-examined over and over. His penance for one stupid mistake.

He tugged a mask over her face and gave her oxygen from the portable canister. 'Yes, I'm sorry, it hurts, it hurts, sweetie. I know. You'll feel better soon.'

He hoped. He watched, and waited. The kid's pulse raced. Her eyes closed...

'Whoa, baby. Come on.' He attached the stickies from the portable monitor to her chest. Fast heartbeat…but a rapid heartbeat was better than none. The swelling was still severe but it often took a while for that to go down.

'Breathe, kiddo. Breathe well. Come on, wee thing.'

'Where is she? Where is she? What the hell happened?' A well-dressed woman burst into the room, ran over and launched herself at Ava.

Cal managed to hold her off just enough to make sure the toddler was coming round. A little sigh then a big gulp of air. A whimper. Then a full-blown cry. Thank God. He breathed out long and hard. 'She's doing okay now, aren't you, little lassie?'

'What did you give her?'

'You are?' The last thing he needed was to be giving out confidential information to the wrong person. He thought he knew who she was, but waited for confirmation.

'Her mother, of course. She's allergic to peanuts, eggs, tree nuts and anything dairy. And they know this. It's in her notes and I have to remind them all the time. They should be more careful.'

'I gave her adrenalin. She's had an allergic reaction.'

'Her EpiPen?' The woman looked down at the

ampoule. 'Not her EpiPen? It has her name on it. What the hell…? This is ridiculous. I'm going to write a letter—she could have died because of their incompetence.'

Now he understood why the teacher had been just a little reluctant to hand over care. Cal stroked Ava's hair again and watched her blink more alert. He turned to her mum, not caring what fuss she was making. 'Now's not the time. She's getting better, but we'll have to take her in for observation. There's a chance she could have a rebound reaction.'

'But the Epi—'

'Let's leave the mystery of the disappearing epinephrine 'til later, right? I totally understand why you're upset, but she's okay now and that's the main thing. We can go over everything else when things are calmer. Now, let's get her to the ambulance. You want to carry her? I can come alongside with the oxygen.'

The mother opened her mouth, appeared to think better of what she was going to say, then nodded. 'Yes. Thank you.'

The ED was busy for a Monday afternoon, but he handed Ava and her very concerned mother over to Stephanie, wishing, not for the first time, that in this job he got to see how his cases panned out. It would be good to see this kid as her normal wee self, playing and giggling, or to see if she was as serious as her mum. But the chances of him seeing any of his cases in anything other than an emergency situation were dwindling with every day he spent here. Just under four weeks and he'd be gone, never setting foot in this place again.

So it was probably a good job he didn't allow himself to become emotionally involved after all.

He was on his way out when he saw her. Actually, he heard her first—that lyrical voice over the beeps and coughs and cries that were the soundtrack of the ED—and he turned to her as if tugged by a magnet.

She was laughing and talking to an old man who she was walking alongside, notes and X-rays in her hand. As if she sensed Cal watching her, she slowly turned and smiled. In amongst the stark, rigid edges of the no-fuss easy-to-clean ED furniture, the sharp antiseptic smells and raw life, that smile added a little softness. She was real and her empathy shone through, even in the most urgent of situations. Strange how his gut tightened instinctively. He wasn't generally one to pay any attention to the state of his heart either, but it definitely sped a little faster right now.

She said something to the man, who looked over at him too, then she walked towards Cal, her dark hair pulled back in a ponytail, eyes bright.

Dancing. 'Hey there, I wondered if we'd ever get to meet at work.'

'It's all in the timing.' A quirk of the universe. A different shift, a busier day and he'd probably never have met her.

'Did you bring little Ava in? I heard she'd had another scare.'

'Yes. You know her?'

'I know her mother. We went to school together.'

'Lucky.' He was too much of a professional to say what he really thought.

'She owns and runs the Mountain View Hotel, which didn't get the reputation for being the absolute best for nothing. She can be quite demanding, so I've heard from her suppliers. I hope she didn't give you a hard time?'

'She's just anxious about her daughter. It's totally understandable. People react differently under stress.'

'Yeah…and the rest. I hear what you're not saying too.' Abbie smiled and shuddered. 'I hope I'm not that kind of mother.'

Not seeing her pregnant made him forget she was having a baby. Surrogacy. They sure did things differently here. Still, he hadn't had a child of his own but had experienced that surging protective instinct, that unconditional love that made people do extraordinary things when necessary. 'You'll love your kid no matter what and will fight for it too; a mother's instincts. One gurgle and you'll be a pushover.'

'Oh, believe me, I'm bad enough just looking at the scans. But you've only seen me on a good day. You wouldn't like me when I'm angry.'

'I'll remember that.'

'Abbie? Can you——? Oh.' The pregnant lady from the café the other day came over, her eyes giving him the once-over. 'Hello.'

'Emma. This is Cal. This is Em. She's my——'

'Best friend. Yes. Hi.' Cal nodded, instantly on his best behaviour. For some reason it mattered what Emma thought of him. He stuck out his hand and shook Emma's.

A strange look passed between the two women. Actually, it was more a flicker of anxiety that fluttered across Emma's face. She quickly hid it and smiled broadly. 'Hi. Abbie told me about the medivac the other day. Sounds a bit wild. Good job you were there.'

'Och, it was a challenge, that's for sure. But we managed, didn't we, Abbie?'

'Absolutely. The A Team, right?' Abbie's smile tugged at his gut. There was something unspoken between them. He'd felt it on the run, too—a fledgling friendship. She was fun and pretty and kind. More than anything she had guts and he admired that.

But there were plenty of women on the planet like that, some of whom lived a damned sight closer to Duncraggen. So why this particular woman in this particular corner of the world seemed to be playing with his head he couldn't be sure.

His phone started to ring. A good excuse to leave now because staying would be foolhardy. Like the date idea. It had been agreed on the spur of the moment, but it was hardly something he could renege on now. 'That'll be another job, no doubt. Right, I'll be gone, then.'

'See you tomorrow?'

'Oh, yes. At the archway. Good.'

He left them to it, unable to put his finger on what it was that he was feeling. Conflicted was the best way to describe it. She was a lovely woman with a whole ton of baggage, none of which he could do anything about. Or wanted to. There was no point in taking on someone else's business, no matter how nice and fun and kind she was.

Hell, he hardly knew her, so taking her out for the morning had been a pretty dumb suggestion. But he was a man of his word, whatever else.

'At the archway?' It was Emma's voice float-

ing over to him as he walked away. 'What's that about?'

He didn't hang around long enough to hear the answer.

Abbie felt like a kid playing hooky rather than a grown-up woman. But she had the distinct sense she was playing hooky more from her promises to Michael than anything else. This was the first time she'd been out with a man since the last date night with her husband. This wasn't a date, it was just a bit of fun, but should she even be here?

Her last words to Michael had been, *'I'll never love anyone like you. I'll never love anyone again.'*

'Of course you will,' he'd said. *'I want you to. I want to leave knowing you'll find someone else to make you happy.'*

She hadn't thought back then that she'd ever be happy again.

Which was all a bit morose given she was in a car with Cal going...somewhere. She looked over at him as he drove, a glimmer of a smile on his face. He was looking up at the mountains around them and in his eyes she could see a kind of wonder and excitement that was infectious. She was probably too nonchalant about it after twenty-odd years living here, but looking from a visitor's perspective...yes, the snow-capped mountains and deep slicing valleys did take your breath away. 'So, where are we going?'

She only hoped it wasn't a bungee jump, given that was the number one tourist attraction round here.

'Can't say.' The smile bloomed. 'It's a magical mystery tour.'

In truth, the whole thing was a mystery to her—the weird flutters when she looked at him, the lightness in her chest that seemed to squeeze back the sadness she'd worn for so long. The fact she was having a physical reaction to a man after all this time. That was pretty intense stuff. Was it real, though? Or was she just being silly? She swallowed back the apprehension and the nerves and tried to keep her voice steady. 'Then I should really be driving, seeing as I'm the local.'

'And then it wouldn't be my treat, would it?'

'Have you done much sightseeing while you've been here?'

'I've seen a lot, but I think you could live here for a whole lifetime and still not see everything. Right?'

'Definitely. I've hardly explored any of it. Bad of me to admit, I guess, but when you live somewhere so amazing you do tend to take it for granted. I've always wanted to do some of the great walks, but never have time. I certainly won't when the baby comes. I'll just have to add them to my bucket list—which is getting longer and longer, I might add.' Michael hadn't written one. They'd been so damned sure he was going to beat the cancer they hadn't wanted to cloud that vision with might-haves and wish lists.

Stop thinking about Michael.

Michael was dead. Cal was very much alive. But it was so hard, after all this time, to stop thinking about her husband. A betrayal of sorts. She looked at Cal's profile, a strong defined jawline, long eyelashes to die for, and her heart squeezed a little. 'So, you said to Marty the other day that you'd like to climb Ben Lomond. Do you do a lot of climbing? Tramping?'

'Hiking, you mean? That's what we call it, but it's the same thing. I used to, yes. But—' He stopped talking abruptly.

'But, what?'

Whatever he was going to say he changed his mind; she could tell by the little shake of his head. He consciously controlled what he was going to say, curling into himself a little. 'Now I just spend my time rescuing people from the mountains instead of scaling them for fun.'

'That's a shame.' She wanted to ask him why, but didn't know him well enough to go probing into his life. Something had happened, she was sure of it. But then, didn't everyone have something in their background? No one got to thirty without some baggage, or betrayal, or loss. If they did, then they were the lucky ones. 'You should really get out there and do what you love. Life's too short to do stuff you don't want to do.'

'You're right there, Abbie. That's for sure. But sometimes you just have to suck up the bad stuff and get on with it.' He pulled the car into a sharp left turn and drove through the huge gates and the entrance to the Lakes Shooting Range.

'Shooting?' How many times had she driven past this and never once stopped? This tourist was showing her around her stomping ground, go figure.

He climbed out of the car and waited for her to do the same, then started to walk with her up a gravel path. 'Abbie, please don't tell me you were the Queenstown Primary top shooter as well as best arm wrestler and fastest woman in the southern hemisphere.'

'Why?'

'You're a veritable superwoman and I'm feeling just a little intimidated by all your achievements.' But he didn't look it as he walked her to the large modern barn advertising shooting and hunting, and held the door open to her. 'Hey, Trent. How you doing?'

Which was Kiwi for *good morning* and sounded strange and quaint with a Scottish brogue.

He was tall and strong and had a confidence she'd always yearned for. She watched as he paid and shook his head at something the owner said, then Cal came over with two shotguns. Shotguns! But he kept hold of them both, refusing to hand one over. 'Before you touch this I need to do a safety briefing.'

'Good, because I've never held a gun in my life. But you clearly know what you're doing.'

'Ah…well, yes. I'm cheating, to be honest. I used to work at a shooting range, part time, you know, after school and in the holidays. I come down here to blast off sometimes.'

'Oh, so you're a world-cup hotshot, then?'

'Not exactly. But not far off.' His eyebrows rose and danced above his eyes, making her laugh. 'Just missed out on the Commonwealth Games in 2006.'

'Oh, my God. Really? You must be good.' Then the penny dropped. 'You really are the most competitive person ever, Callum Baird. You only brought me here because you knew you'd win.'

'Er… I seem to remember it was you who started the whole race thing on the lake path.'

'Me?' But she had. And it had been fun, just like this. Like him.

Once outdoors they walked to a cordoned-off area where there was a machine housing what looked like coloured clay plates and some banked areas called stands apparently, where they did the shooting. After he gave her a thorough safety briefing and she'd been so put off by the dangers of a loaded weapon she almost didn't want to actually hold the gun, he pointed her towards a cluster of trees.

He was standing very close behind her as he helped her adopt the right stance. So close, she was aware of his scent, much more than in the car. It was fresh and wholesome—soap, citrus shampoo. Male. And she was so busy breathing it in that she was barely concentrating on his words. Plus, being so close was making her hands shake a little. Actually, a lot. His voice whispered over her neck.

'Put your ear defenders on. Stand a little forward, leaning on your left leg. That's it.' She really, really wanted him not to touch her thigh like that. Or rather, she realised, with a shock, that she did want him to touch her thigh like that. And more. His words were fuzzy, but that was more about the way she was feeling than his accent. 'Okay, the clay is going to come from the left. Trace it with your gun. Then, try to get a little ahead of it and just as it's about to dip, squeeze your finger. And shoot.'

Whoosh! The clay was out high in the sky and crashing down to earth before she'd been able to breathe. She followed it, right down to the grass. 'I'm rubbish.'

'No, you're not. You just have to stand still. Concentrate.'

How the hell was she supposed to concentrate with him standing so close? 'Show me.'

'No. You do it.'

'Show me.' She nudged him and moved out of the way, offering the loaded gun.

He shrugged. 'Okay.'

Taking the gun from her, he placed the edge of it high on his collarbone, his cheek resting on top and… Bang! A shower of pink clay floated to the ground. Bang! And again. Bang! And again.

'Wow! You're really good.'

'I know.' His forehead crinkled a little. 'Actually, I should have asked. How are your hands? Are they still sore from the gurney? I should have brought you to do something different.'

'I don't think it's my hands that are holding me back, to be honest.' She held her hands out and showed him the rough healing skin on her palms. There were traces where the handles had gouged holes, but on the whole they were heaps better. 'Yes, they still hurt a bit, but not enough to hinder me. I can do that all by myself.'

'Then you've no excuse, woman.'

He handed the shotgun back to her. It was warm where his cheek had been and she tried really hard not to think of him in any way as a sexual, sentient being. All she knew was that she felt strange when she was around Cal. Strange and new and scared and excited and yet comfortable, all at the same time.

'You just have to steady yourself. Be mindful—that's all the rage at the moment, ye ken? Be in the moment. Breathe in. Focus.' A whizz and another clay shot into the air. They watched it together and she tried to trace it as he'd told her. It started to dip. He shouted, 'Shoot.'

Bang!

She let her arm relax as the clay hurtled to earth, intact. 'Whoa.'

He was all attentive, his eyes dark with concern as he took the gun from her and propped it against the stand. 'You okay? Loud? Did you hurt your ears?'

'No. Not at all. But when I hold the gun up my heart's racing and my hands are shaking.' But she knew it had nothing to do with shooting and everything to do with him. He was making her nervous, making her shake. Which was silly. He was just a man. A very good-looking and lovely man. An almost medal-winning shooter. A very accomplished... Her gaze moved from his eyes to his mouth. A very accomplished kisser? Where the hell had that come from? *For God's sake. Stop it.* She did not want to kiss this man.

Any man. But definitely not this one. *Focus. Be mindful.* 'It's harder than it looks. I don't think I can stay still for that long.'

'As I thought.' He stroked his chin and pretended to peer closely at her. 'I diagnose…ants in yer pants.'

Despite herself she laughed. She hated that she couldn't hit the damned target, but, well, he made failure very funny. 'It's hard. I can't slow. I never slow. I'm much better at running.'

She filled her spare time doing things so she didn't have to think too hard about her life. About the empty space in her bed. In her chest. About a future where she was the only parent the baby would have… Oh, yes, she had Emma and Rosie but, when it came down to it, she was going to be on her own. Every night. Every day.

Every night.

And that hadn't really concerned her until now. She didn't want to be alone.

Although, she wasn't thinking Cal would be the one to stop her being lonely. He had a one-way ticket out of here. So she wasn't investing in him. And, anyway, she'd have the baby to fill her every waking moment and no doubt most of her sleeping ones too.

He placed his hands on her shoulders and looked into her eyes. 'Settle. Take some breaths. That's it. Slow right down.'

'Okay.' She shook out her arms, made them loose and relaxed, did the same with her legs. Stretched her neck from side to side. 'I'm good. Okay. Let's do this.'

He gave her the gun and once again corrected her stance. Stood by her as she watched. Focused. Boom! Shot.

The clay fell to the ground. Intact.

Give me a break. Concentrating and breathing slowly were not happening with him so close. 'Cal, could you just step back a little?'

'Sure. Whatever helps.' There was a light in his pupils, a tease that tugged in her gut.

She was going to show him, if it killed her. She could do this. He was not having an effect on her. She would not let him. *Breathe. Don't think about him. Focus.* She closed her eyes and focused on her heartbeat. Opened them again. Caught the clay in her sight. Traced it. Anticipated the dip and— 'Shoot! Yes! Yes!'

The air was a fizz of pink powder.

'Yes! You did good.' He wasn't quite jumping up and down as she was, but she could tell he was impressed. There was a grin on his face the size of Lake Wakatipu. 'Do it again. Show me it wasn't a fluke.'

'How dare you? It was skill, not a fluke.'

It was a fluke.

The next clay crashed to the ground. And the

next. 'Aargh. This is so frustrating. I did it once, I'm going to do it again.'

'You will. It takes practice. You've just got to keep going and going. You've so much grit you'll get the hang of it.' He stood back, but then bit his bottom lip and grimaced. 'Oh, and by the way, I have a confession to make. I…er…lied.'

'About?' Her heart jumped to warp speed. She couldn't imagine what he was going to say.

'About the Commonwealth Games. I was nowhere near good enough. Not even a little bit. Not even Duncraggen best. Well…maybe Duncraggen best.'

'Aargh, you.' She shook her head but laughed as she swatted his shoulder. Because…yes, she wanted to touch him. 'Why did you lie?'

Because she had when she'd met him?

'Just to see your face when you discovered I might be better than you at something. Priceless.' He went to tug her ear defenders back on, but paused. And then the strangest thing… The atmosphere went from funny to serious in a nanosecond. His thumb trailed along her jawline then across her cheek to her lips. His gaze became heated and focused on her and he smiled. Sexy and more. She knew what he wanted and she wanted it too. A kiss. She wanted to feel his lips pressed on hers.

Holy moly. She wanted to kiss him.

The air stilled. Her heart thundered in her chest and she felt the need to run, hard and fast...away. But she was rooted to the spot. She couldn't move if her life depended on it. She just wanted to see those eyes looking at her so intensely. To feel his mouth on hers.

But then his eyes darkened further, as if a cloud passed through his thoughts, and he took a step back, cleared his throat. 'Right then, lassie, you have about twenty more cartridges. Let's make them count.'

CHAPTER FIVE

HE'D ALMOST KISSED HER. Within an inch. Closer. He'd almost broken his promises; that nothing and no one would get in the way of looking after Finn.

And yes, he'd had some flings with women who were of the same mindset as him; who'd just wanted a good time, no questions asked. But with Abbie, things were different. She was the kind of woman who'd want more than just sex. Who was the whole package deal with a kid on the way—the *love of her life's* kid—and when Cal was with her he wanted a piece of that too. Something he hadn't ever contemplated. Something that was tugging hard. But he just couldn't. It wasn't in his future any time soon.

He had a debt to pay. And if it took a lifetime then it wouldn't be long enough.

A waitress brought over two glasses of pinot noir and placed them on the table, then fussed around finding blankets for their legs. Sitting

outside to admire the view of rolling hills covered in vines had been a great idea, but didn't
account for the cool wind whipping round them.

When the waitress had finally gone, he tipped
his glass against Abbie's. 'You did well. I'll be
phoning the New Zealand selectors and recom-
mending you for the shooting team.'

'As if. I think you might need to hit the target
more than fifty per cent of the time to qualify,
right?' She laughed. She was wearing a thick,
baggy, candy-striped woolly jumper that hid
most of the gorgeous body he'd seen on the run
the other day, and skinny jeans tucked into knee-
length brown boots. She looked the most relaxed
he'd seen her, her hair in loose curls and her dark
eyes sparkling. Always moving. Always dancing. So alive that he couldn't help wanting her,
wanting a piece of that vibrancy too.

'It's early days. I'll have you shooting like a
pro in no time.' And why he'd said that he didn't
know. One minute he was making the decision
to loosen the ties with her and the next he was
making more plans with her. He was starting to
lose the plot.

'Not sure I'm going to give up the day job just
yet, though—' She tipped her glass against his.
'But, thanks. It's been fun.'

'That was my aim. Pardon the pun.'

She pulled a funny face. 'Oh, God, you're as bad at jokes as you are at running.'

'I told you, I let you win.' Tactics. Truth was, he'd already run fifteen kilometres that day and had been on his way back to town when he met her. Running to the bridge again hadn't exactly been on his agenda. But he'd never been one for backing down from a challenge. Especially not from someone like Abbie.

She was tapping her fingers on the table. Brewing something. 'Okay, so the score is one all. I won the run. You win the clay shooting. What should we do next? Something that neither of us are good at, or something we both are?'

He spluttered into his wine glass. 'I think you'll find I'm good at most things. Some things I'm exceptional at…' There was an edge in his voice that took the conversation from sweet to spice in an instant. Strange thing was, he couldn't control it even if he wanted to. He looked directly at her now, at her eyes and the perfect bow of her mouth. She swallowed. And again. But she didn't stop looking right back at him, too.

She licked her bottom lip and heat shot through him.

He'd almost kissed her and he still wanted to.

She leaned forward a little. 'I was talking about physical stuff.'

'So was I.' Because, why not test the waters?

He'd assumed she was all about the kid and the package, but maybe not. Maybe she, like him, wasn't looking for anything deep. One last fun fling before motherhood hit.

His suggestion hung in the air and her cheeks coloured a deep, deep red, then a full all-out body blush. Cute. So, he made her feel a little of what he was feeling, then. Good to know he wasn't going mad and that there was definitely a mutual attraction here. It was just a very stupid idea. Seemed you couldn't break a habit of a lifetime. He was, after all, in his brother's words, the king of stupid.

He opened his mouth to say something about getting physical together, but the moment was broken as the waitress came out with their food.

Dragging some sweet mountain air deep into his lungs, he calmed himself. Thank goodness he hadn't actually proved his brother right. For one crazy minute he'd almost blown it. Abbie wouldn't want a fling. That had been his feral red blood talking, not his sensible educated brain.

After demolishing a huge helping of venison pie and salad she put her knife and fork down and leaned back in her chair. 'So, I've thought of the perfect thing. How about we climb Ben Lomond next week, then? I reckon I can just about fit you in on my next day off. Before things get really baby-crazy.'

'Absolutely not.' The words were out before he could temper them. Truthfully, the thought of being up there on that ridge in the snow made his heart sing. But up there, *with her*, being responsible *for her*, turned the song from melody to high-pitched scream in his head. Not a chance. He softened his voice, relaxed his hold on the wine-glass stem. 'Hiking? In this crazy, unpredictable weather. No, thanks. You saw what happened to Marty, why we were up there in the first place. If we went up on our own there'd be no helicopter, no radio out.'

'But we'd be more prepared and there's two of us. I've been up it a thousand times, I've run up it in the summer in just trainers and a T-shirt. It's not that bad. Marty was just unlucky. Hell, you can get killed crossing the road. You can die—' She blinked. Swallowed. Blinked again. 'Well, you can just randomly die and there's no rhyme or reason for it.'

He knew she was talking about Michael, and he got that, but it wasn't going to change his mind. 'All the more reason to be sensible, then, especially with a baby coming.'

He'd thought that might put her off, but she became more animated, her hands open and moving, palms upwards. 'I want my child to be outgoing and adventurous, not to be afraid to take risks.'

'Taking risks is all very well until you have to live through the consequences. Not so exciting and life-affirming then, believe me.' He was not going to talk about this any more; they were steering into dangerous ground. Too close for comfort for him.

But she ran her forefinger round the rim of her wine glass, her mouth forming a pout, and he wasn't sure if she was angry or teasing or frustrated. 'What's really the matter, Cal? Are you fobbing me off? No? What is it, then? Scared?'

Of losing someone else? 'Actually. Yes, I am.'

That was so not what she'd expected him to say.

There was a moment of confusion as she reconciled the excitement in his eyes at the mention of tramping and then the shut down at the suggestion he did it with her. The grip of fingers on the wine glass and tightening of his jaw. 'But I thought you loved it.'

'I do...did.'

He wasn't exactly forthcoming, so she pushed a bit more. 'Scotland must be one of the best places for hiking. Did you climb Ben Nevis?'

He nodded. 'Sure. Me and just about everyone else in the UK. It's like a motorway in summer. Dangerous in winter, and unpredictable, just like here, the rest of the time.'

'I've never been, but it's a lot like here, though,

isn't it? I've heard people say the South Island reminds them of the Highlands.'

'Yes. Similar in lots of ways. Lots of hills…' He took a deep breath and let it out slowly. 'There's this thing, a challenge for hikers; any mountain in Scotland over three thousand feet is called a Munro. There are nearly three hundred of them. The challenge is to summit them all. It's called Munro *bagging*. You can combine two or three in one day, others are multi-day walks just to get to the top of one. Others you chip away at one day at a time. Some are on the tiny islands in the Hebrides, some are hard scrambles, others are more gentle. Like I say, you're supposed to get to the top of them all and tick them off the list. All two hundred and eighty-two, to be exact.'

'Wow. I thought New Zealand had a lot of hills. And have you completed them all?'

He nodded, pride evident in the straightened shoulders and tilted jaw. 'I have. Twice, and then…well, I haven't finished the third completion.'

'I can see from the way you're talking that it's something you love.'

'Aye. But I do it alone these days, if I go at all.'

'Why?'

He tugged at the zip on his padded black

jacket. Up and down. Up and down. 'Because that's how I like it.'

'Isn't that dangerous? More dangerous than if two of us go? There's safety in numbers, right?'

His foot was tapping against the table leg. 'I'm fully prepared and equipped. I don't take unnecessary chances. I know the risks. It's better if I go on my own.'

'Better for who?'

Cal stilled completely and held her gaze. 'For me. Look, I'm not having this conversation with you, Abbie. We are not going walking, tramping, hiking or anything up that mountain or any other mountain, okay?'

'Whoa. Bossy sibling alert.' No one had ever spoken to her quite like that. But he was deadly serious and there was no budging the man on this, clearly. 'Okay. So, no Ben Lomond.'

'No Ben Lomond. Not until the summer anyway, when there's less chance of horizontal winds and snow. Then, you can do what you want.'

'But you'll be gone by then.'

'Aye. I'll be long gone by then.'

There was a sudden wistful pang in her chest. 'Why do you go on your own?'

'I climb the mountains because I have to. Because I can't not. I love it. But I go on my own, at my own pace. Those are my rules.' He drained his wine and stared out across the vineyard.

She probably shouldn't have pushed it further, but she did anyway. Because—well, hell, there was a story there, on the tip of his tongue, and she was going to find out what it was. Maybe it would explain why he wanted to be the Lone-bloody-Ranger up on those hills, and why the shut-down thing occurred every time she asked a question. 'What happened?'

His eyes were fixed on the table, right hand curled into a fist. 'You don't want to know.'

'You mean, you don't want to tell me.'

'No. I don't.' Cal sighed low and deep and shook his head, and she knew she'd overstepped the mark.

'It's okay.' She reached over the table, took a gamble and wrapped her hand over his. Because she'd pushed him to an edge and she didn't want to watch him dive over it just because she wanted to get to know him better. 'I'm sorry.'

He tugged his hand away and sat up straight. 'Ach, it was in the papers, you can have a read if you want to be bothered. Short version is: we were on a ridge and my brother fell. A long way. He's…not the same as he was.' He drained his glass and she got the distinct feeling that the subject was closed. His eyes had dimmed and he wore a cloak of pain so intense she thought he was going to shout or rage or storm off. But after a couple of moments he gave her a smile that was half reassurance and half sadness. 'Let's get you back to town. Two o'clock, wasn't it?'

'Cal? Wait—' She wanted to apologise for pushing him into such a dark place, but he stood up and was striding over to the counter to pay. How terrifying to have a brother suffer so badly and still to wear the strain of that. All she wanted to do was stroke Cal's back and try to make things better for him.

Which made her stop in her tracks and take a moment to think.

Everything inside her was screaming not to get involved with this man. He played a dangerous game. He took a gamble with his own life while dedicating his time to saving others. He was fun and deep and sexy and stirred the sleeping dragon inside her. There were more butterflies in her stomach now, flexing wings and stoking a heat inside her. And she knew, if she wasn't careful, that heat might just burn her.

So, sense said it was better not to get involved with Callum Baird at all. But the more she got to know him, the more she wanted to know.

Emma was waiting outside the antenatal room, tapping her watch as Abbie half walked, half ran along the corridor, ignoring the *Do Not Run* and

Slippery When Wet signs tacked to the walls. She wasn't exactly frowning, but it was a close-run thing with her pinched mouth and theatrical sigh. 'Two-oh-three. It's not like you to be late.'

Abbie grimaced. The last thing she wanted was for Emma to think she wasn't committed to this. She pushed all thoughts of Callum Baird and his roving thumb and mysterious past to the back of her mind. This was her future. Right here. In that blossoming belly. What the hell she'd been thinking, spending the morning playing, she didn't know. She'd been a fool to let him distract her from real life. 'I know. I know. Sorry. Sorry. Things ran late. I hope we're not the last.'

'There's a few in there already, but Sally's not here yet and she's the one taking the tour.' Emma held the door open and they squeezed into the crowded room. Women of all shapes and sizes stood around chatting. There were a few men, too, but certainly no match to the number of pregnant women.

'At least it's not all couples,' Emma said out of the corner of her mouth as she surveyed the others. 'Some grandmas here too, by the looks of it, and friends, girlfriends. At least we won't look odd being two women together.'

'The invitation said birthing partners. I don't care what anyone thinks. Mind you, if they start showing any birthing videos I may have to leave.' She was joking, of course. She'd delivered enough babies to know exactly what happened.

But Emma took the bait as Abbie knew she would. 'Hey, this is your baby. You're going to be there watching me suffer whether you want to be there or not.' She was laughing, but Emma didn't take her eyes from Abbie's. She had that no-nonsense look on her face that Abbie knew from years of being her friend. If she wasn't mistaken they were just about to venture into Emma interrogation territory. 'So, what's he like?'

Strike one for Abbie. 'Who?'

Emma rolled her eyes. 'Come on. *Outlander* guy.'

Abbie turned her back to the other class members and walked her to the window, all the better to chat a little without being overheard. Queenstown was a small enough place for gossip to spread between the locals as it was. How was he? Where to start? 'He's okay. I guess.'

Another eye-roll. 'Oh, please. Neither of us have had a date in years and all you give me is *okay*. Really? Really? This is so different from your first date with Michael.'

'Because it wasn't a date.'

'Yeah. Just like I'm not looking like a huge beached whale. How did *whatever it was meant to be* go?'

It had been a date.

There was no way of dressing it up in anything other than that. It had been a date and she'd enjoyed herself with a man. Really enjoyed herself, to the point of wanting to kiss him.

'Well…' It was fun stalling, just to see Emma's third eye-roll in as many minutes. 'On the downside he didn't turn up in a kilt. But on the upside he took me shooting. Like, a real gun. Clay things. I even hit some.'

That got a rise of the eyebrows. 'Interesting.'

'That's what I thought. A strange place to take a girl on a non-date, or even a date-date.'

Emma grinned. 'A rugged man like that looks more like the action type. Mountain biking, skiing…'

'Yes, well, having seen the way he moves in crampons I'd say that too.' Abbie fought the shiver that ran through her, wishing it were caused by the memory of the ice and not of him. 'He said he used to do more tramping but stopped. And then he went quiet, like he was dealing with memories.' And she knew all about that. She'd been there after all. Still was there in some ways.

But she'd decided to put Michael in a box and determined not to talk about him to Cal. Her chest tightened at the thought of that. It was hard to leave her former life behind. Hard to think of someone else filling Michael's shoes.

Not that anyone could. But maybe it was time to start moving forward. Baby steps.

Emma wasn't letting up at all. 'Sounds like Mr Scotland has a few secrets, then.'

The injured brother. The ridge. 'Hmm. I don't want to pry.'

'Really? Of course you do.'

Abbie giggled. 'Yes, of course I do. But I know I shouldn't.'

This elicited a smile from Emma that was warm and encouraging. Which wasn't exactly helpful. 'You have a strange look in your eye, Abbie Cook. And I'm not sure what that means.'

'It means I had a nice morning with a nice man, that is all. I probably won't see him again. In fact…' She made a decision right there and then. 'No. I won't see him again.'

'But that look does not say nice, or that you don't want to see him again. It says interested.'

'I'm not interested.' *Liar.* 'He's heading back to Scotland to care for his injured brother.'

'Oh, be still my beating heart. The man's a saint, too.'

Abbie thought about the way his thumb had skimmed her lip and the look of desire in his eyes. He'd wanted to kiss her. Not very saintly at all. 'No. No, he's just nice.'

'If you say so.' Her best friend shook her head, then looked suddenly pensive. And protective. The way Abbie had seen her in the past when saving herself and her daughter from a painful relationship with Rosie's dad. She tucked some of Abbie's wayward hair behind her ears and smiled, softly. A look that said she knew what Abbie was feeling. That more hurt was not needed, for either of them. The message telepathically delivered through kind eyes and a gentle touch. *Don't get in too deep.* And then in words. 'Just be careful, eh?'

'I don't need to be. It's nothing. Just a bit of fun.'

But Abbie wanted so much to tell her about the near-miss kiss and how looking at Cal gave her a fit of butterfly stretches so hard it made her tummy tickle. And how she liked the way he smelled. She wanted to be back being sixteen again, the two of them piling into her bedroom, jumping on the bed and spilling secrets. *Did he put his arm around you? Open-mouth or closed-mouth kisses? How did he taste? How far did you go?*

She wanted the innocence and hopefulness of youth to wash through her, instead of knowing what she knew: that falling in love was lovely, but all it led to, in the end, was falling apart.

And she couldn't have that. Neither of them could.

The class leader bustled into the room and grinned as they took their seats for the introduction. 'Excellent, ladies and gents. I'll just go over the plan for the afternoon…'

It was all such bad timing. Emma had never thought she'd look at another man again and think…nice. She'd never thought she'd go on another date. Or start to heal her broken heart. Or that she wouldn't be able to tell her best friend for life the way she was feeling because she didn't want to break the spell. She wanted to hug this feeling to herself.

But also, she didn't want anything to come between her and Emma and the baby. They were a tight-knit little family, with Rosie. That was what they'd promised each other, after Alvin had gone, and after Michael.

So she said nothing and grabbed a chocolate biscuit from the table next to her and Emma smiled, and they were fine.

But Abbie wasn't.

Then the woman running the class clapped her hands and they were up and off on the tour, talking about birthing pools and gas and air. What to pack in the maternity overnight bag. When to call, who to call, what to expect.

A quick look in the labour suite, then an equally

quick exit as a woman was wheeled in in a wheel-chair, screaming, 'I need to push. Now!' And the red-faced man with her asking for a vomit bowl. For himself.

For a moment the group stood in silence, eyes wide and slightly panicked. Swiftly followed by little hiccups of giggles.

In another suite, a brand-new baby had recently entered the world and let out a hearty little cry that completely broke the panicked spell. And they all grinned. Emma glanced over at Abbie and her eyes widened. 'Feeling a little bit more real now?'

'Oh, yes.' There was nothing more that Abbie wanted than to be here, heavily pregnant with Michael's baby. But being here with Emma was a very close second best.

'Well, feel this too. Kicking. Your baby's a little soccer player.' Emma grabbed Abbie's hand and pressed it against her belly, as she'd done when she was pregnant with Rosie. There was such a softness in her eyes that Abbie thought she might cry.

'Oh. Oh, my goodness. So he is.' There was a raw thickness in Abbie's throat, but her heart felt light and fluttery. This was real. This was what she'd wanted for so long, what she'd endured days of pain and injections and interventions and heartbreak for. This baby.

This was what they had to look forward to.

And she wasn't going to let a sexy, blue-eyed Scotsman—saintly or otherwise—get in the way of that.

CHAPTER SIX

'THIS IS ERIC. He's eighty-four and was involved in a motor vehicle-versus-truck accident over in Wanaka. Took a knock to the right side of the head on impact. Neck tender at C-three and four. Right chest and shoulder sore from seat belt. Suspected fractured right tib and fib. Right ankle was crushed so it took a little time to dig him out. He's shaky and shocked but holding a decent BP all things considered. He's had pain relief and is feeling a wee bit better if he keeps still. Moving's the tough bit, eh, Eric?'

Abbie would know that accent anywhere. Her heart flipped as she turned to see Cal in his red overalls and hi-vis. That voice had been distinctly absent for the past week and she'd decided, resolutely, that if she heard it again her heart would absolutely not flip.

Traitor.

She'd also decided not to look up the Scottish ridge accident on the Internet, even though she'd

typed his name more than a dozen times and let
her fingers hover over the return key. It wasn't
her business and she wasn't about to start nos-
ing around behind his back. If he wanted to tell
her, then that was fine. If not, well, that would
have to be fine too.

The old man on the trolley looked familiar,
although with the neck brace and facial bruis-
ing it was hard to tell. A quick glance at his
surname and she knew they were neighbours.
'I'll give you a hand through to Resus.' She nodded at Steph, taking the end of the gurney and
wheeling him through, Cal following. Their patient was frail and shaking as she put her hand
over the paper-thin skin of his knuckles. 'Eric,
it's me, Abbie. From the apartments at the end
of the road.'

'Eh?' Pale blue eyes darted to her and she
thought he might just have relaxed a little bit.
Good. Healing happened a lot more quickly if
the patient wasn't fighting the whole time.

'I fed your cats when you were in last time.
Remember?'

Eric patted her hand. 'Good...girl.'

'You've had a bit of a bump.' Glancing at his
vital signs on the paramedics' mobile monitor,
she could see he wasn't out of danger, and she
was glad to have something to focus on that
wasn't a Scotsman with a nice smile. Still, she

wished it hadn't been someone she knew who'd had a head-to-head with a logging truck; Eric was lucky to have come out of that talking. 'This is Stephanie and there'll be a doctor through any second and they'll get you sorted out. I just wanted to say hi and that you're in safe hands.'

'Thanks.' His hand was cold and weak and she gave it a squeeze, found a blanket for him and started to attach him to hospital monitors.

Once she'd explained he was headed for immediate surgery and a long stay she whispered to him, 'Don't you go worrying about the cats. I'll pop round and feed them until you're home. Don't worry, I'll sort them out. Key in the same place?'

'Thank you. You're gold, you know that, Abbie?'

Cal's eyes met hers across their patient and he smiled and nodded.

She shook her head and laughed. She wasn't gold, she was just doing what anyone else would do in the same situation. But she felt like gold bathed in Cal's smile.

Nixon, the ED consultant, bustled in then Cal left and she focused entirely on her patient's care and not on the memory of that smile and the tingle skimming across her skin.

'I'll get straight onto the orthopaedic surgeons.' After doing a quick assessment Nixon picked up the phone. 'In the meantime, we'll get more fluids into him and keep him comfortable with more pain relief. If you're a neighbour, do you know his next of kin, Abbie?'

'No, but he's been in before, so it'll be in his notes. A son, I think. In Dunedin.'

'Excellent.' Nixon finished his call and gave her a quick smile. 'Hey, I just wondered…how's Emma doing?'

Unexpected. 'She's fine. Getting a bit tired these days. Why? Is there a problem?'

Nixon shook his head and his face flushed a little. 'No. No problem. I was just… Nothing. It's okay.' And with that he picked up the internal phone and started dialling. Conversation closed.

She watched him for a minute and tried to work out what that had been about. Then she heard the dulcet tones of the ward clerk and the auxiliaries discussing the love lives of one of their colleagues and decided he was probably concerned about her being the subject of gossip. Or, more likely, concerned about her pulling her weight at work. Or…then the Arrest Code alarm went off and she put everything else bar saving lives to the back of her mind.

Later, as she was pulling on her coat at the end of her shift, she felt the little hairs on the back of her neck prickle and awareness ripple over her.

Cal was close somewhere; she could sense it. Sure enough, he was outside the staff café talking to the helicopter pilot.

She was going to try to sneak past and not allow her fluttering heart to take charge, but her words tumbled out before she could stop them. 'Hey, Cal.'

He ambled over, all smiles that sent ripples of need over her skin. 'How's young Eric?'

'He's a lot more comfortable now he's back from Theatre.'

He fell into step with her as they walked out into the bright sunshine. Queenstown was putting on a very summery attempt with a gentle warmth and pretty flowers in huge barrels along the pavement. Cal slipped on sunglasses that at once elevated him to rock-star status. 'Do you often take on the feeding of other people's animals when they're in hospital? You don't have to do that.'

'I know, but it's a small place, you know. We help each other out when we can.'

'I know all about that. You can't sneeze in Duncraggen without someone handing you a tissue. Where are we headed, by the way?'

She hadn't a clue, in all reality. 'I'm going to the primary school to pick up Rosie. I don't know where you're going.'

'Home, I guess. I'll walk with you to the school—my car's parked nearby.'

'So you can regale me with the tale of Eric's rescue along the way?' And it felt stupidly and refreshingly normal to walk side by side across the car park. It was these little things she missed: having someone to talk to about what to have for dinner, the sweet peck on the nose for absolutely no reason, a hand to hold in the middle of the night, walking across a car park. Hell... she really hadn't realised at what point grief had turned to loneliness, but now she felt acutely that Cal had slashed through all of that. He was filling her up with good feelings, but also turning the loneliness into a longing. A longing to be touched, held, kissed, and she wasn't sure how to deal with that.

After he'd talked about cutting Eric from the car he asked, 'You got to your appointment in time on Tuesday?'

'The visit to the maternity ward? Yes, thanks.'

'How was it? You learnt how to have a baby?'

She laughed, thinking about that poor man and the vomit bowl and his wife or girlfriend who was in the throes of labour. 'We've been there before. Emma's got a five-year-old—hence the school—so we know the drill. We have the birth plan and everything all agreed on.'

The walk to the school took them past a little

park that smelt of fresh spring blossom. Magnolias hung full and ripe and pink from spindly branches. Cal didn't seem to notice any of it, maybe because it was just plain old pretty and not stunning snow-capped peaks. He seemed much more focused on her impending parenthood. 'That must be interesting. I mean, what if she wanted something—drugs, or whatever—and you didn't agree with that? How does all that work? Who's in charge? This surrogacy thing raises a lot of questions, doesn't it?'

'Like, whether she'll even give the baby up? What if there's something wrong with it? Will I still want it? Yes, I know. It's very complicated and wrought with questions and ethics. But bottom line, she's helping me out and we know each other well enough to know how we feel about most things.'

Emma was the only person who really knew what Abbie was going through, but it felt good to be able to share these thoughts—thoughts she'd kept away from Emma for fear of upsetting her—with someone removed from the situation. It felt a little disloyal, but he was a good sounding board, just letting her get her jumbled thoughts out without judging her.

Whatever he thought about the surrogacy setup he didn't say, and she couldn't read it from his body language, but he seemed to take it in his stride. 'Something I've always wondered… Does she…do you pay her?'

'No, it's an altruistic surrogacy. I'm not allowed, legally, to pay anything but her expenses.'

'And then, afterwards…how do you see that panning out?'

'She'll always be involved, obviously. She's my friend and she's already brought up one baby—I'm going to need all the help I can get with that. Good thing we live next door to each other.'

'What if you didn't, though? What if you decided to move… I don't know, to the other side of the world, for example. Or Australia. Or even Auckland?'

They'd come to a halt as a taxi pulled away from a taxi rank. Abbie pressed the pedestrian crossing button and they waited for the red light. She was fighting the urge to slip her hand into his and feel his heat on her skin. 'I would never move. I couldn't. How could I? I'm the mother, but she's so involved. It wouldn't be fair to any of us to be separated. Why are you asking?'

'Ach, I was just interested in how it all works.'

'Queenstown is my home. I have my…memories here. I could never leave.'

His eyes softened as he looked down at her ring. 'Michael?'

She rubbed her finger. Would she ever take

this off? Could she? 'Not just him. Everything I've ever known is here.'

Cal shrugged, scrubbing a hand through his hair. 'I couldn't wait to leave Duncraggen. I wanted to see the world. Rule the world, if I'm honest. I was a cocky wee bairn, I have to admit.'

'But you went back.'

He stiffened. 'Of course. He needs me.'

How? Why? Maybe if she just looked on the Internet she'd know...but no. She was going to resist that temptation. It was his story to tell, if and when he wanted to. 'Now you rule your small piece of Duncraggen.'

There was a wink and a rueful grin. 'Well, Finn believes he rules it, to be honest...but I just let him think that.'

Abbie unlatched the school gate and dipped in to pick up Rosie. There she was, all pink-cheeked and a mass of dark curls causing the usual squeeze of Abbie's heart. What this kid had been through, and been protected from, sometimes haunted her. Out of all the men in the world, Emma had somehow fallen for one of the bad ones. Ever since, she'd determined that the only person she was going to love unconditionally was her daughter. Oh, and Abbie... and their bun in the oven. Abbie wondered if she could possibly love her own child any more than she loved Rosie, and decided that that kind of love was simply unimaginable.

'You can have five minutes to play before we go home; either the play park here, or the one near the house. One, Rosie. You can choose.'

The little girl's eyes narrowed as if she had to make a life-or-death decision. She looked over towards the park and the shiny slide, so much higher and better than the one closer to home. The choice was hardly difficult. 'This one.'

'Good choice. But no tears when we go past the other one.'

'Okay, Abbie.' Her eyes darted towards Cal. Luckily, with a couple of uncles close by, Rosie had had a lot of positive men in her life. 'Who's that?'

'A friend of mine. This is Cal.' Friend. It felt strange saying that, but that was what they were. Nothing more.

He was leaning against the gate, hands stuffed deep in his pockets. He tugged one out and waved at Rosie. 'Hi!'

But the little one had lost interest and was careening towards the slide.

What had they been talking about? Oh, yes. Finn. 'So, how is your brother?'

Sighing, he shook his head. 'Don't even ask.'

'Not climbing mountains without your permission again?'

He grimaced, shoulders stiff. 'Planning a ski-ing trip. With one leg. I ask you.'

Rosie slowly climbed each step, putting both feet on each rung as she went. Finally at the top she gave a little wave. Her smile splitting her face.

'Hold on with both hands, sweetie.' Abbie waved back and nodded encouragingly for her to sit down. Sweet, sweet girl. Then turned back to Cal. 'You can't protect him for ever.'

'Why not?'

'How old is he?'

'Twenty-seven.'

She coughed, dragging her eyes away from little Rosie and back onto him. Childminding and chatting was serious multitasking. 'Really? From the way you were talking I thought he must be under eighteen.'

He shrugged. 'You think I'm overprotective.'

'I think you love him very much and don't want him to get hurt again. But it's his life, Cal. Let him take some risks.'

'But what if…?' He shook his head. 'I know, I know. Well everything's easy in theory.'

How to say this without sounding hurtful? 'I don't know what your relationship with your brother is really like, okay? But I do know that when you hit adulthood things aren't as basic as limiting a five-year-old to this park or that park. Your brother sounds like he was a pretty competent athlete before his accident, so I'd say he's trying his damnedest to get back to some semblance of that. To get his life back. You want that, right?'

'Of course. Yes, of course I do. But what if he—?'

He couldn't say it. He couldn't imagine it, and she was glad he hadn't had to face that kind of thing as she had. But, for Abbie, it was getting easier to say these things. It had been something that she couldn't shy away from when reality hit. No amount of euphemisms would change the facts. 'What if he dies? Then he'll die doing something he loves.' She put her hand on his arm and looked up at him, hoping he'd take this with as much kindness as she meant. 'Let him live again, Cal.'

'It's not that easy.'

'I know it isn't. Believe me, I do understand. You want to wrap them up in cotton wool and save them from pain and hurt. Let me tell you something—' She dragged in a deep breath. This wasn't something she shared often, but she hoped it would help. 'I spent so long trying to make Michael better, chasing cures and looking up miracle treatments on the Internet, that I forgot about spending good times with him. I just wanted him well so we could restart our life. I couldn't think about the alternatives. But all I ended up doing was alienating him, pushing him to do things he didn't want to do, trying different remedies, making him feel worse in the end, making him fight when he didn't want to fight any more, when he was tired of all that *brave* talk. All he wanted was to spend his last months doing fun things and being surrounded by love, but I was on a crack hunt for a cure and couldn't rest until I found one. It wasn't him who didn't have a bucket list, it was me who wouldn't let him.'

'You were only trying to help, you were fighting for him—that's a good thing, isn't it? You loved him and fought for him.' Cal nodded then as the penny dropped. 'I see. Yes. I get what you're saying. It's his choice.'

'Life's too short to force people into corners. I think, if I could, I'd just try to support people chasing their dreams...even if I didn't think those dreams would work. Even if they sound like a really rash idea.' She hoped it didn't sound like a lecture. 'And I need to apologise for last week. I tried to make you talk about things you didn't feel comfortable talking about.'

His hand covered hers and his thumb stroked over her skin. Such a simple gesture, but it stoked something deep inside her. Something more than lust. Although there was a good deal of that there too. His voice was soft when he spoke. 'And I should apologise for ruining a great morning with my *greeting*.'

'Greeting?'

'Whimpering. Whining. You know, carrying on.'

'It was nothing.'

'I'm not good at this.'

'You are.' She could have looked up into those eyes for hours. So demonstrative, so clear and bright. There was a funny feeling she got when she looked at him that she'd never had before. Or at least, she'd forgotten it. The keen ache down low. The straining of her breasts for his touch. The crazy ideas that popped into her head, the hope, the feeling that maybe things could be better.

She'd forgotten, or hadn't wanted to remember. God, she'd forgotten how that all felt and just looking at him it seemed almost in reach. Her eyes drifted to his mouth and she wondered… could she? Could she reach up there and put her lips on his? How would that feel? How would she feel deep inside? How would he taste? Would he kiss her back? Did he want to?

There was a little cry. Her name. Abbie turned and saw Rosie with her hands on her hips. 'What is it, sweetheart?'

'See-saw, please.' She pointed to the large

plastic seesaw, each end shaped like a bright blue horse's head, the mane twisted into a handle for little hands. 'Okay, then. Two minutes on the horses.'

After a couple of moments of her bouncing up and down off her heels, Abbie's eyes naturally sought Cal out again. She was drawn to him, like a magnet. *Like a stupid infatuation,* she told herself.

It would all blow over when he headed back home. He was still watching and smiling. Waving. He must have thought she was dreadfully dull and domesticated, but this was her life and she was looking forward to more of it, not less. But instead of looking bored he looked actually quite animated.

Eventually she managed to convince Rosie it was time to go home for dinner, but as they came through the gate he said, 'I've had a thought about our next dare. If you're still willing?'

She tried not to look too pleased at the prospect, but her heart kicked up a little. Dare not date. She liked that idea. It sounded a lot less committed to a path she couldn't take a single step on. 'Maybe?'

He leaned in, his finger curling round a strand of her hair, and whispered, 'How are you in the saddle?'

Her gut clenched and fizzed and she giggled.

Like a teenager. Grow the heck up!

'In truth…rusty.'

'Excellent. Me too.' He grinned. Winked. 'Day off?'

'Thursday.'

He was still very close, his nose in her hair, mouth very close to her ear. Warm breath skittered over the back of her neck, making her shiver. 'I'm on an early. Meet you at our usual place at three-thirty?'

Our usual place. Her heart rate doubled. And she was probably reading far too much into it all. She grimaced, unsure as to what to do. Her heart screamed yes, but her head was being far too sensible. 'But—?'

Far from being playful, he was kind and genuinely concerned. He drew back and looked at her. 'What's the matter? Scared?'

She nodded, resisting the urge to curl into his heat and his touch. Scared didn't begin to describe how she was starting to feel when she was with him. 'A little, to be honest.'

He tipped her chin up and for a moment she thought—*hoped*—he was going to kiss her. But that would have been foolhardy with little eyes on her and a tiny chubby hand tugging her to *go home now, Abbie.*

He smiled. 'Don't worry. You know enough

about me by now to be confident I'll make sure you're safe.'

But that was the problem. Given the way her body was reacting to the tiniest of touches and the slightest flirt, she wasn't sure her heart would ever be safe around him.

CHAPTER SEVEN

THURSDAY COULDN'T COME around quickly enough. The work Cal had been so invested in, and the training he'd come here to do, barely held his attention these days, only enlivened when his thoughts drifted to dancing eyes and loose dark curls. Things he did on his day off, rather than things he spent the majority of his time doing. For a woman who he'd only seen a couple of times, she was seriously starting to get under his skin.

The thought of not being here gave rise to a weird feeling in his chest. And he knew he shouldn't take it out on his brother, but he felt trapped by one world when part of him wanted to be in another just for a little bit longer.

Having arrived at the archway early, he was taking the opportunity for a catch-up. And beginning to regret it. 'What I don't understand, Finn, is why the hell you're bothering to ask my advice? You're hell-bent on killing yourself, so just go off and do it.'

That was what Abbie had suggested he do, right?

Let them follow their dreams, she'd said.

And okay, he knew he wasn't handling this well.

Finn was stretched out on the sofa in their lounge at home. It was the middle of the night there, so curtains were drawn. Ever since the accident, he'd had difficulty sleeping and often rang to while away the dark hours. Behind him, Cal could see the detritus of his life: dirty cups, beer bottles, pizza boxes. A stack of laundry. Books. The wheelchair. Fidget, the cat, sat aloof on its seat cushion; the only sentient being that used it these days, after Finn refused to sit in it ever again the day he came back from the rehab ward. Against medical advice, obviously.

That was how he was, how he'd always been; an independent, single-minded, beat-the-odds kind of guy. Somehow his whole life had been preparing him for the accident. His eyes rolled. 'Ach, you could at least listen instead of rage at me. I want you to come skiing with me. A week in Austria.'

'And watch you kill yourself? No, thanks.' But actually, he'd sworn to do whatever it took to get his brother a life, so he'd have to do this too. And enjoy it, for Finn's sake. Maybe Abbie really did have a point about supporting his dreams—instead of smothering him with overprotection. 'When is it?'

'February.'

'February? I won't have accrued any leave by then. You know this trip is taking most of it.'

'You'll be able to scrape a few days, though? Look, if you don't want to I can find someone else to come.'

February in Europe meant cold and sleet and snow. Here in New Zealand it meant the height of summer. Cal looked out across the lake, imagined what it'd be like here. Imagined what she'd be like in the summer. Those curls hanging loose over naked shoulders. Swimming, sun-kissed. Holding her baby. Being a family.

The brakes went on that thought as his chest squeezed tighter. He'd no more envisioned a family—a baby, and someone else's baby at that—than he'd imagined himself flying to the moon. But recently the scenario had started playing in his head…a maybe, a what if. Which was all kinds of weird and unsettling.

He looked at his brother and remembered cradling him in his ice-cold arms, and the promises he'd silently made back then. And how he'd begged him to hold on and told him he'd do everything—absolutely anything—to help him live. And if that meant giving up any kind of future for himself, then so be it.

These two halves of his life weren't going to gel any time soon. And, above all of that, whatever he wanted didn't matter. He owed his brother, he'd promised him and he was sticking to that. For ever. 'Nah, I'm with you, mate. Every step. Remember? Every. Single. Step. Sorry I've been so down on you, Finn. I'd like to blame jet lag or something, but I'm—well—'

He wasn't going to mention Abbie because that would only complicate things.

'Just a moody bastard?' Finn smiled. Something of a rarity these days, especially in their conversations. The break had been supposed to help—absence making the heart grow fonder, and all that. He wasn't sure it had.

'Yep. Okay, you got me. I'll make it work. Skiing, eh? I'm looking forward to it already.' He'd make sure they stuck to the nursery slopes, even though he knew Finn would make a beeline for the moguls. Suddenly his senses fired into action and he knew she was here. Before he turned around to see her and gave his game away to his know-it-all brother he stood up. 'How's everything else working for you? Maggie bringing food in? Pete still doing the morning and evening shifts?'

'Aye. It's smooth. I told you it'd work. The

timetable you made is a dream and I get some peace and quiet when they've all stopped fussing.' He didn't need to add, *unlike when you're here*, but it hung there between them.

'Good, well, I'll be back soon enough, irritating you and cramping your style. But I'm going now. I've got things to do. I'll call you in a couple of days. Email me the details of the trip and I'll forward it to the boss.'

'Hot date, is it?' Did the guy have an X-ray into his head? 'What's she like? Knowing you, she'll be blonde and well…developed.'

He cringed. How much of this could Abbie hear? He lowered his voice. 'Going horse riding.'

'Lucky you.'

He was. He knew that. Having two working legs was damned lucky. It could just as easily have been him who'd fallen from that mountain. 'There are plenty of places that could help you go riding. Everything's possible these days. We can get you on a horse if you want, when I get back.'

'I meant the date part. Scars might be hot these days, but I'm not sure false legs are up there in the Top Ten Sexy Body Parts lists.'

'Finn…' There was a time when Finn had literally had women queuing up for him. When being the scrum half for the Swans had been a big deal. When he'd earned the country's yearly annual wage in a month. 'It'll happen.'

'Yeah. I can't move for hot women wanting a piece of me.' Finn rubbed a hand over the two-day stubble on his chin and pulled a thick wool blanket over his shoulders. 'Go. Have fun, you big idiot.'

'And you, ya *bampot*.' And things were back on an even keel again. God, he missed him. But he wasn't about to let him know that.

'Bad timing?' Abbie was leaning against the grey stone wall that edged this end of the lake, a little distance away, obviously giving him space to chat to his brother. She'd tied her hair into a long plait that fell over one shoulder, a half-circle of another tiny plait framing her face. She was wearing those skinny jeans from the other day and a navy-blue padded sleeveless jacket over a pale pink sweatshirt. She looked horse-riding ready, but he wanted to skip that bit altogether and take her straight to his bed, peel those clothes from her and run his mouth over every inch of her soft-looking skin.

God, keeping his wicked thoughts—never mind deeds—to himself was going to be damned hard.

He walked over to her, resisting the tug to wrap her in his arms and, instead, giving her a chaste wee kiss on her cheek. She smelt of apples and something flowery and the tug intensified. He stepped away and pointed over towards his car. 'Just climb in. Actually, I took your advice about supporting him and things weren't too bad.'

She laughed. 'I'm looking forward to hearing you say things are good.'

'You might have to wait a while. Right, let's get going, Calamity Jane. Did you remember your cowgirl hat?'

Her eyes glittered. 'It's been a long time. I think I'm going to need something a lot harder than that.'

'I'll see what I can do.' He wasn't sure what to make of her statement, whether she was playing with him or was woefully innocent of the reaction she'd achieved low down in his gut. Her perfume filled the car, a sweet softness that had him hot under the collar. Somehow he was going to have to keep that burning heat under wraps, while the thought of skiing in Europe left him colder than the snow he'd be sliding down.

'Horses are always so much bigger than you think they are.' Abbie leaned her head against the warm equine throat and stroked the chestnut nose of Kelly, her ride for the afternoon. There was something very soothing about a horse's deep breathing. And God knew, she needed all the help she could get with Cal around. The hard hat made her look a bit silly, but she didn't mind;

Cal had one on too and he looked gorgeous. 'It's been a while since I rode, so please tell me she's a good-hearted soul.'

Bryn, the woman who ran the stables, gave her a reassuring smile. 'She's a sweetie and very used to nervous riders. I'll be coming along, so we'll keep an eye on you.'

'And what kind of route do we take?' Cal was up on his bay horse, Boss, looking as if he'd been born to do this. And, no doubt he was a champion horse rider or something.

Bryn flicked the reins towards Abbie and nodded at her to climb up onto the step, grab the reins and then hoist herself into the saddle. 'Just a meander through the farmland and then down along the riverbed. Nothing too strenuous, unless you want to gallop—there's space down there to let loose and Boss loves a good run.'

'Let's take it slow and see how we go. I haven't ridden in a very long time.' Abbie jabbed her heel softly against Kelly's side and clicked her tongue against her teeth. 'Come on, girl. Walk on.'

They filtered into single file; Bryn up front, Cal second and Abbie taking up the rear as they made their way from the farmhouse, downhill, to the forest. It was cool and fresh down there, an eerie glow bouncing off the tree bark covered in moss, as if someone had washed the view with a green filter. There was little noise save for bird-song and the clomp, clomp, clomp of hooves.

This had been a great idea; a chance to unwind and force her muscles to relax in a different kind of exercise compared to what she was used to. Abbie breathed deeply, all the better to steady her head, taking note of the altogether nice view of Cal's back. The man had fine posture. Great shoulders. Her eyes moved lower. A gorgeous—

He turned and gave her a wave, pulling to a halt and waiting until she'd caught up with him where the path widened enough for two. 'You okay there?'

Why did he have to be so considerate? It just made her like him more. 'Yup. Just plodding, as I like it.'

'I thought you'd be galloping ahead, blazing a trail.'

'Kelly and I have only just met. I don't want to push her too hard. Later, maybe, at the river.' She ran her hand down the soft coat and patted, receiving a little whinny in reply. 'This is lovely. You really do know how to spend a day off.'

'Just trying to make the most of things. I hope we didn't mess with your schedule? Whoa, wait, watch your head.'

She bent at the sight of a low-hanging branch coming towards her just a little too quickly. 'Wow. Thanks. I do prefer having two eyes. Although I do feel very guilty being here when I should be painting the nursery and…well, doing adult stuff. Nesting. But I don't have the hormones to kick me into action, so I'm just putting up with Emma's periodic nagging.'

'All in good time. You're allowed a little bit of fun before the parenting thing kicks in.'

Was she, though? If she wasn't carrying this baby the least she could do was be ready for it when it arrived. 'I have so much to do.'

'You've got a few weeks before Christmas. Plenty of time. Besides, how many times have you heard new parents say they could never be prepared for what hit them?' He grinned at her wide-eyed response. 'How are you feeling about it all?'

'Excited. Nervous. Scared. It doesn't seem real to me, even though I know it is.'

'Yes, it would be weird seeing her carrying your child.'

That was exactly how she felt. Weird. Excited, nervous, amazing, and…weird. 'I can't quite believe it. It's almost like seeing her pregnant with Rosie again rather than with my baby.' Then, the truth of it fell out of her. 'I hope I love it. I mean… I will, of course. But what if it doesn't bond with me? What if he or she wants Emma and not me? What if we don't get along?'

He let out a low sigh. 'Of course you'll love each other. Of course he'll love you.'

'You think it's a boy?' She had no idea, alternating between the genders depending on the shape of Emma's belly, what her cravings were and what Abbie secretly wished for: a daughter. And then, sometimes, when she saw a little boy kicking a ball, or charging breathless around the play park, she wanted one of those too.

Of course, Cal didn't know any of this; no one did. She had no one to share her crazy higgledy-piggledy thoughts with. But given they made little sense, maybe that was a good thing.

Cal looked nonplussed. 'How would I know? I just couldn't imagine having a baby girl. I'm not sure I understand the female of the species too well. Mind you, given my brother, I'm not sure I know a lot about the males either.'

'I've been reading a lot of "what to expect" books and have followed the pregnancy from being two little lines on a stick, every moment, every scan, every ginger biscuit for morning sickness. Emma knows what she's doing. She'll help me.'

If we're still friends at the end.

Truth was, Emma hadn't given Abbie one single hint that she wasn't happy doing this. But you just never knew, did you? In the end? Guilt rolled through Abbie again. Here she was riding a damned horse and Emma was waddling around work, looking after Queenstown's injured, carrying a baby, thinking about how she was going to entertain her five-year-old later.

How could she ever repay her?

The route opened up to rolling hills covered in tussock grass, past an old dilapidated shed and duck pond, then downhill. Abbie remembered to lean back a little to stop her from falling. It was a long way down to hard earth.

Cal's eyebrows rose in question. 'So, you've got no family around, then?'

'None here.'

'They're where?'

Abbie thought about her parents, who'd given her the choice to move overseas with them back before she'd even met Michael but she'd waved them off on a mid-life adventure never thinking for a moment how alone she'd end up being. 'They semi-retired to a little village in the South of France. They have a small bed and breakfast there and three apartments here. The one I live in, next door where Emma and Rosie live, and the one on the end of the block. They rent the end one out as a holiday let, and use it when they come home. Which is getting less and less frequent. They've really got into the ex-pat lifestyle in Europe and the weather helps Mum's asthma.'

'You must miss them.'

'Of course. Especially…when Michael… Sorry, I shouldn't keep talking about him.'

Cal shook his head, giving no emotion away, certainly no frustration. 'You don't, not really. He was a big part of your life. I understand.'

She wasn't sure if he really did or was just being kind. Because he wasn't exactly going to tell her certain subjects were out of bounds, was he? 'So, anyway, yes… What with a new baby and getting ready for Christmas, I have lists coming out of my ears.'

Callum shifted in the saddle and peered closely at her head. 'No. Nothing there that I can see.'

'Okay, smart guy. My phone's stuffed full of lists, I'm nowhere nearer putting up a tree or anything and yet here I am with you. Again. Playing hooky.'

'It's my animal magnetism. Women just can't resist it.'

If she could have swatted him she would have; as it was, all she could do was tut. Loudly. 'Don't flatter yourself, Mr Baird. I'm only back here because I don't want to show you up. Otherwise I'd be off in the wind, galloping across the grass.'

'Sure you would, honey.' He grinned, holding the saddle and rocking forward and back on his horse like a cowboy from a film. So sure of himself, so confident. So damned—

He interrupted those thoughts. 'Why did you

tell me—that first time, I think it was—that you didn't like Christmas?'

'Oh, you remember that? Well… Christmas always used to be a big thing for me and Michael. He loved making things magical for me. Then…' She swallowed at the memory of how they'd known that the last Christmas was going to be exactly that. So she'd gone all out to make it special and it had been. Nothing could beat that, the little cocoon of intense emotion. 'Then it was just me. And it kept on being just me. Of course, I had lots of invitations to go out and Emma made me talk to people and socialise at some point. Last Christmas I spent in hospital after a miscarriage. A failed IVF.' She wasn't sure if she should have said anything because Cal seemed to close down a little at that. 'Sorry, too much information?'

He shook his head. 'No. Not at all. You've had it tough, Abbie. I'm sorry.'

'Not your fault.' She didn't tell him about the other four miscarriages before, during and after Michael's illness. The IVF, the waiting game. The hopeful Christmas songs that made her feel as if her heart was breaking. 'Anyway, let's not spoil this day. All that's in the past.'

'Aye well, the past has a way of hanging around a bit, doesn't it?'

She determined to throw off this air of sadness and so she made herself smile and breathe in the fresh air. 'No. Not today.'

Up ahead Bryn had stopped and was waiting, but Cal waved her on. 'We're good, thanks! We're fine.'

She waved back, then started to trot on towards the almost dried-up riverbed covered in gravel and stones, and a small beach area. When they caught up she rubbed her hands together. 'Okay, you two. You're doing very well. Cal, you say you've ridden before?'

'Aye.'

'And, Abbie? You used to ride?'

'A bit, yes. I can trot and canter a little.' She didn't want to think about how long ago it was. She was hardly a pro, but she'd aced pony club when she was seven.

Bryn pointed forward. 'Well, the river stretches on for miles and it's like this all the way to a small wooden bridge. When you get there wait for me, okay? I'll keep back and make sure you're okay. Whenever you're ready.'

Cal raised his eyebrows. 'Ready?'

No. But she wasn't about to let him see that. A good gallop would shake off the doom and gloom that she'd introduced into the conversation. What they needed was another race. 'Any time, mate.'

'Yes, because I can see from your white

knuckles that you're very relaxed and ready to gallop.'

She opened and closed her fingers, then grabbed the reins again. 'Like I said, I'm just getting back in the saddle.' And if that didn't sound like a come on, she didn't know what did. 'I mean…'

'I know exactly what you mean.' There was a tease in his eyes and he laughed. 'How do you feel about going just a little bit faster?'

'Fine, I think.'

He reached out and stroked her arm, his eyes intense. 'Okay, just relax and stop thinking about all the things you should be doing and everything that's happened before. Just enjoy this. This moment. Live in this moment—or whatever thing you're meant to do.'

'Okay. I'd never pegged you for New Age, but okay.'

'Great. Relax. Breathe in. That's right. Excellent. In again. Out. And…race you!' He kicked hard and sped off, disappearing in an arc of water that curled high around him.

'Hey!' Typical! Always trying to out-run or out-shoot or just plain beat her. Laughter bubbled up from her gut and she squeezed her ankles against Kelly's flank. 'Come on, Kel. Let's go. Let's show him.'

It was like flying. Well, a bit soggier than flying, but with the wind in her hair and spray on her face she felt the most alive she'd felt for years. This was absolutely the best way to spend a day off. Freedom from thinking about anything but the moment. And Cal.

Yes, Cal.

He was standing in the stirrups now, one hand raised in the air, a loud cry of something joyous splitting the air.

So she stood up too, raised her hand and was just about to scream when Kelly stopped. Just stopped. And lowered her neck.

The next moment Abbie was falling forward and somehow sideways and tumbling and there was no way she could stop it. The great hulk of horse seemed to shift, or Abbie did or something, and the ground was rising up to her, too fast. Too fast.

Reaching her hand out, she tried to ease the impact but her bones bumped and crunched onto gravel and stones and water. All breath was pushed from her lungs and she felt the impact reverberate through her like shock waves. She wanted to cry out, but there was no air. Just pain. A sharp pain in her left wrist.

And right then—in that moment that she had been so concerned about living in—she realised what an utter idiot she'd been. What a risk she'd taken.

Because how could you look after a newborn baby with a broken arm?

'Abbie! Abbie! Are you okay? Hell.' She heard the thump of hooves and the splash as Cal dismounted. But she didn't want to look up and see him because that would admit to all the rules she'd broken. How stupid was she? Why would she do something so reckless?

He was by her side, kneeling in the shallow water as if it didn't matter, and then looking at her as if she really did. His hands ran over her face, down her shoulders. 'What happened? Where do you hurt?'

'It's nothing. I fell, that's all. She just stopped. I don't know why.'

He turned to the horses and caught the reins that were dipping into the water, tied them around a large rock. Then he turned back. 'Let me look.'

She didn't want him to look, didn't want to look herself. Because it would only scream how irresponsible she'd been. She could feel the prick of tears. Humiliation. Guilt. Shame. But most of all because it actually bloody hurt.

But instead of looking at her wrist he kept on looking into her eyes. 'You're not okay at all.'

'I am.'

'Stop being brave and come here.'

The next thing she knew she was pressed

against his chest, his arms tight around her. He
was hot from riding, his breathing hitched. His
hand clasped the back of her neck, stroking her
hair as he whispered soothing noises and words
that seemed to reach into her heart and tug so
tightly she wanted to cry even more. 'You'll be
fine, wee lassie. You're okay. You're safe. It's
okay. It's okay, we'll fix you up.'

But she wasn't okay at all. Because the longer
she stayed wrapped here in him, the more she
couldn't bear the thought of tearing herself away.
Everything hurt; every bone and sinew in her
left hand, every riposte she shot at herself was
like a knife jabbing at her. She was stupid and
foolish and reckless and what kind of an almost-
mother did that? What kind of a responsible person would take such a risk?

But she was also a woman. A widow.

A *woman*.

A woman whose only thought right now was
that she was in the arms of a good man. A sexy
man, hell, not just sex on legs, but gorgeous and
kind, and who stirred something deep inside her.

She'd been through enough heartache to last
her for the rest of her years, and was going to
devote all her energy to her child when it came,
so she deserved just one moment in the arms of
a strong man.

So she let her body be lulled by Cal's heat, let

her mind be hypnotised by his voice and she lay
her head against his chest and breathed him in.
Breathed in a man who wasn't her husband, who
wasn't the father of her child, who wasn't someone who could offer anything other than comfort right here and now. But she didn't care; she
wanted that. Just a moment where she could be
a woman who was being comforted, protected,
cherished. By a man like Callum Baird.

Suddenly she realised her heart was raging
fast and it wasn't from the fall. Her body was hot
and buzzing, but not from the exertion of exercise. The stroke of his hand on her back made
her press harder against him. Her mouth was
wet and yet dry. Her breathing fast and unsteady.
Like her thoughts. She liked this. She liked him.
She wanted him.

'Hey.' He edged away from her, holding her
shoulders, tugging gently. 'Are you all right?'

'No. No, I don't think I am.' She closed her
eyes, suddenly unsure. Did he want her the same
way? And then what? Kissing him was a one-
way ticket to heartbreak.

But she wasn't sure she could stop it either.
She opened her eyes and touched his cheek, ignoring the sharp twist of pain that shot up her
arm. This was one moment she was going to
take for herself and to hell with broken bones
and broken hearts.

He was so close, his gaze on hers, the heat there mirroring the way she felt. He wanted her. She didn't need to ask. 'Where do you hurt, Abbie?'

'Here.' She touched her heart, feeling raw and exposed and turned on all at the same time. 'Because I'm going to kiss you and I don't know what will happen next.'

He sighed and laughed and ran his thumb over her lip in that way of his that made her knees buckle. 'Well, let's find out, shall we?'

CHAPTER EIGHT

IT WAS NO USE. He couldn't resist any more. There were too many emotions swirling in his chest and all of them were because of her. For a moment he'd thought she'd done some serious damage, then it was just relief she was alive and okay, and then hot on the heels of that the sharp tang of need.

Cal lowered his mouth an inch from hers. Seeing the desire in her eyes, but a struggle there too, almost broke him. 'Abbie, are you sure?'

Because, despite all the bravado, he had no idea what the hell was going to happen either, or even what could happen.

The struggle was still there as she nodded and edged towards him, but it had been overridden with longing. He cupped the back of her neck and tilted her mouth towards his, his reservations exploding into a thousand pieces the second his lips touched hers.

There was a tentative moment that was almost

innocent exploration, then she opened her mouth to him and he couldn't stop the very *un*-innocent groan coming from his throat. His mouth slid against hers as sensation after sensation pumped through him. She tasted of the mountain air and fresh river water, so good. So damned good.

Her hand snaked around his neck and she shifted in the water until they were both on their knees, pressed together, his palms cupping her face. Her scent was all around, and he couldn't get enough of it. Of her. There was something about her that tugged and tugged and tugged at his heart, at his groin.

At his heart.

He deepened the kiss, seeking out her tongue as a heat started to build inside him. This was what those little games had been about; the races, the give and take, the push and pull, dancing around what was so inevitable—that despite every single sensible reason not to, everything would lead to this. *This.*

His gut contracted at the feel of little beats of pressure as her soft body pressed against him, a perfect fit in his arms. There were so many things he wanted to do to her, and with her, right now he could barely think straight. He slid his hand down her neck, down the side of her jacket and under her jumper, a riot of stars bursting in his head as he touched the soft skin there.

But then she was pulling away, breathing fast, and there were tears in her eyes that she was trying to blink away.

He wasn't sure his heart would be able to take much more. There was something about her that made him putty in her hands; he would give her the world, just for another kiss. To kiss those tears away. 'Are you okay?'

'My arm.' She was cradling it in her good hand. 'I think I've done some serious damage.'

'What? Let me look.' He'd been kissing her while she was hurting and needing medical attention? Stupid bloody fool. Then he wanted to curse loudly as he took her hand and saw her wedding ring glinting in the sun. All desire leached away. At least, in his head, anyway. In his gut he still wanted her. In his heart he still wanted her. But wanting her was a hiding to nothing. She had more baggage than anyone else he'd met—apart from him. 'You always seem to get hurt when I'm around.'

'It'll be okay. It's nothing, I'm sure.' She gave him a smile, but it seemed a little wobbly and unsure and he couldn't help wondering if she'd looked at her wedding ring and thought the same thing he had. Or whether she was just in pain. 'I hope it isn't broken. The last thing I need is a plaster cast and a new baby.'

'Could make things interesting, for sure.' That

hadn't even occurred to him. He was going to say the cast would probably be off by then and that he'd help all he could, when he remembered he couldn't. There was a thundering in his chest. What a big mistake this whole thing had been.

'Ahem.' It was Bryn. God knew how long she'd been standing there; he hadn't heard her approach and she was on foot, leading her horse. 'Sorry to interrupt, but are you okay?'

Wincing, Abbie jumped up, water dripping from the knees of her jeans. She held up her hand, which was swollen and starting to colour in deep purples and reds. 'Kelly wasn't in the mood for a runabout. She clearly just wants to eat.' Abbie nodded towards the horse, who was tugging at the tussock grass with her large teeth, oblivious to what she'd just done. 'But I think I might need an X-ray on my hand.'

Bryn's eyes widened. 'Oh, my God. I'm so sorry. Are you okay? Only, I wasn't sure and I didn't want to…er…interrupt.'

Because we were too busy making out when we shouldn't have been.

Cal's chest constricted. He'd kissed her without thought for anything other than that moment.

Kissed her.

He wrapped an arm around Abbie's shoulders, making a mental vow to look after her, but not to start any more kissing or…anything else. There were too many reasons not to. 'We just need to get her out of these wet clothes, and then down to the hospital.'

'No problem, let's get you back to the farm and we can take it from there.' Bryn took hold of Kelly's reins and handed them to Cal. 'Abbie, can you manage to get back on? Do you want to?'

She was shivering now. Shock. Cold. Passion? That had taken a very definite downturn. 'I don't know. But I guess it'd be quicker if I did.'

'Absolutely, we've come a long way and it's an uphill hike home. There's a boulder over there. If we walk Kelly over you can climb up onto her again—if you're sure? She's a real plodder usually. That's why I give her to the less experienced riders. I can't imagine what she was thinking.'

Abbie gave a wry smile, her shoulders sagging a little. 'She was just interested in the grass, and I was propelled forward. I shouldn't have been standing up in the saddle for a start.'

And that was his fault. He shouldn't have been messing about; he should have been much more concerned about her welfare instead of charging ahead. One slip. One slip was all it took. It wasn't as if he didn't know that. He should have been paying more attention. Should have protected her.

That was another reason why he couldn't do any more kissing; he was dangerous to be around.

Bryn called over, 'Can you help, Cal?'

'Sure thing.' The only thing he wanted to do more than help was rewind the whole morning. The taste of Abbie was still on his lips and hers were red and swollen. Regardless of what he'd vowed, there would be no forgetting that kiss. Ever. It was the best thing that had happened to him in his whole sorry life. He gave Abbie a hand to mount the horse, making extra sure she was safe and secure and out of his reach. 'Come on, Abbie. Up you go.'

'I have clothes you can borrow.' Bryn took her phone out. 'Do you want me to call ahead and get Tane to phone someone?'

Cal bristled as he fashioned a sort of sling from his T-shirt, then wrapped his jacket around Abbie's front, pulling her good arm through the sleeve and zipping her in, hoping to help her get warm. He was going to sort this out. 'No. Really, I'm a paramedic, Abbie's an ED nurse. We just need to dry off and get back to town. We know what we're doing.'

But after the kissing and the wanting to do it all over again, even though he shouldn't, it was clear, without a shadow of a doubt, that they didn't have a clue.

* * *

'Stop fussing, please. I'm fine.' Of course it had been Emma that was the first one to see them as they walked into the ED, red-faced and bruised and still a little damp and dishevelled. Of course it had been her who had filled out the forms and shaken her head and given her that teasing naughty-girl look behind Cal's back, along with her *hottie* and *phwoar* looks and the thumbs up, as if they were really sixteen again.

So, of course, it was Emma who was now trying to get Abbie to take more painkillers and elevate her arm on cushions in Emma's apartment. Rosie was fast asleep in bed and Cal had gone home. Been sent home, actually, because there wasn't anything more he could do and Abbie needed some space to get her head together. Which was difficult given the analgesics she'd already had.

The memory of the kiss had lingered between them as she'd looked for words to say to him on the drive from the stables and hadn't been able to find any. What could you say after one smouldering kiss that had ended so abruptly?

It had lingered as they'd walked from the car to the ED making polite conversation and as they'd sat waiting in X-Ray and not even made real meaningful eye contact.

But something had changed between them and

she thought it was right about that moment he'd looked down at her hurting wrist and seen her wedding ring.

'It's a nasty break, and even with a plaster cast on you still have to keep it higher than your heart to help the swelling go down.' Emma stopped plumping more cushions and frowned. 'I know, I'm teaching my grandmother how to suck eggs. But you need looking after and I wasn't sure whether you wanted Cal to stay on. Plus, once he was satisfied you were going to be well looked after and that he could come back tomorrow, he didn't seem all that keen on staying. What's going on there? Horse riding not quite the perfect date after all?'

'It was a dare, not a date. And it was great. Really. Lots of fun…until the fall. I'm worried about what I'll do, when the baby comes, with a cast on.'

'You'll manage. *We'll* manage. But I get the feeling it's not just your arm that's bothering you.'

'I'm fine. Really.' Thing was, Abbie just didn't know how she felt about the kiss and she didn't want to tell Emma about it for so many reasons. It was so hard to even begin working out what she was feeling. Yes, it had been divine. Yes, it had made her want him more. Yes, he was perfectly perfect in every way and made her heart thrill completely. But…well, he wasn't going to be around and she'd had her fill of getting attached to men who didn't stay.

Worst thing of all: she didn't want to get attached to Callum, but she actually thought she probably was, just a little bit. Even a little bit was too much.

'Well…' Emma rubbed her large belly and rocked from one foot to the other as if trying to get comfortable. 'Missy's certainly been active today. I think she wants to join the fun out here.'

The painkillers didn't dull Abbie's panic. 'But you're only thirty-six weeks. I'm not ready. She's not ready. We're nowhere near ready.'

'Hey, calm down. She's just been doing somersaults, that's all. She's got lots of time to cook yet.' Emma grinned and sat down next to her on the sofa. 'So, without wanting to pry too much, I really do want to know what's going on.'

'With Cal?'

'With Cal. I don't want you getting hurt. I mean, getting your heart broken…given that you're already in physical pain.' Marriage for Emma meant pain. Men, for Emma, meant pain. Physical as well as emotional. She'd been hurt badly by a man who'd used her to get what he wanted. Commitment and love weren't ever really in the picture.

Cal wasn't like that. 'It was just an afternoon out, that's all.'

'Hey...' Emma grabbed a cushion and held it against her chest. 'You remember when we were kids and we used to imagine what our lives were going to be like and we said we didn't need princes to make us princesses?'

They'd been six or seven and had had the whole of their lives to look forward to. It had been very straightforward back then; girls ruled. Girls could surmount anything. Anything at all. Including a dead husband and an abusive one. If only they'd known what the hell was going to hit them. 'I most certainly do remember.'

'Right. So, then we discovered that princes could actually be quite good fun. And then, well, then we learnt that nothing is ever perfect. Thing is, we've been through a heap of stuff together and I really do want you to be happy...' There was a soft mist in Emma's eyes. She was a strong, independent woman, but she had a squishy heart. 'I can see he makes you happy. You have a look, you know? You seem excited by him and that's amazing. I love to see you like that; it's been so long. Too long...'

She squeezed the cushion tighter against her chest and Abbie wondered if there might be a little bit of envy there, or at least a fear of being left alone, pregnant and not horse riding with gorgeous Scottish men. Or any men. But no, surely not. Cal wasn't going to be a permanent fixture; Emma knew that.

There was still a little ache in Abbie's heart at the thought of the kiss. 'He's a nice guy and we had some fun, but that's all.' If she said it out loud she might actually start to believe it herself. Then, the words just tumbled out. 'We kissed.'

Emma clapped her hands together. 'I knew it. Or at least I guessed.'

'Can I not have any secrets from you?'

'No. Don't you ever dare. Do you like him?'

'I do.' The pain was starting to break through now and Abbie lifted her wrist and looked at her fingers. They really were a kaleidoscope of colour. 'But he's not worth spending time on, right? I mean, there's no point getting attached to someone.'

'Because of the brother.'

'Callum takes his responsibilities very seriously, obviously. So, to him, I'm probably just a dalliance, a Kiwi fling.'

'He could be your Scottish fling. A Highland fling! God, I'm funny!'

'Seriously? You're suggesting this just before I become a mother. With a broken wrist.'

Emma shrugged, then smiled. 'Good point. Probably not one of the best ideas I've had.'

Oh, but it was. For a few moments Abbie had

been wrapped in his heat and it had been heavenly. She smiled to herself, hugging that thought close. At least she had the memory of one amazing kiss with Cal to see her through to old age. 'So, I'm going to call a halt to it all. I don't want another relationship. I don't want to think about anything else other than my baby, my family. Me and the little one.'

'Are you sure?'

'With him around the place I can't give the pregnancy or anything else my full attention.'

Emma patted Abbie's good hand. 'You don't have to. I've got this.'

'That is not the point. You're doing enough. Being a mother is everything I've wanted and dreamed of for years, you know that. I don't want to be distracted.' *Or feel guilty about you.* She sighed. It had all seemed so uncomplicated before she'd climbed into that helicopter. 'I like having an easy life.'

'Life isn't easy when you have kids, trust me. But it's your call. If I were you, I'd have a bit of fun. You might not get another chance for a while. This way you get to play a little, no strings.'

'Would you, though?'

'I might.'

'You wouldn't. I thought you were completely off men. With who?'

The smile Emma gave her was wistful. 'No one really… Sometimes I get lonely. Sometimes I think it would be nice to have a little play.'

'No! I thought you were sworn off men for ever?' But that didn't stop men asking after her, though. Abbie still wondered about the subtext of the Nixon conversation, but shoved it away— it wasn't her business and she knew that, after the nightmare of her marriage, Emma was still bruised emotionally. Trust would be hard earned with that woman.

But her friend laughed. 'Hey, a girl can still window shop, right? There are some good-looking men around and I appreciate looking. Or maybe it's just my hormones playing up. Still, if I had the chance, maybe I'd be tempted by a hot man like Callum.'

'But then what? What if I fall for him?'

Emma looked at the arm in a cast propped on the cushions and smiled softly again. 'Honey, I think you already did.'

CHAPTER NINE

THERE WAS SOMEONE knocking at the door.

Was there? Had she dreamt it?

There it was again.

Abbie dragged herself from the drug-induced sleep and sat up, her neck sore and her arm buzzing with pain. She looked around, wondering for a moment where she was. Then remembered she'd left Emma's last night for the comfort of her own bed rather than sleeping on the sofa.

Picking up her phone, she checked the time. Nine twenty-four! She'd slept fitfully but had fallen into a deep sleep after more painkillers in the early hours.

Another knock.

She climbed out of bed, pulling on her kimono-style dressing gown—tugging the sleeve hard over the cast—and walked through to the hall, trying to peer through the bubbled glass, but she could only make out a shape.

'Hello?' She opened the door and her stomach fluttered. The usual response she had to Cal. There he was, his lovely mouth smiling broadly. Those teasing eyes with their laughing, glittering with concern. His gaze ran the full length of her body, taking in her bare legs and navy silk pyjama shorts peeking out from her robe. When his eyes locked with hers there was so much heat there she was at risk of catching fire. There was no way she was going to be able to forget the kiss and the way it had made her feel, no matter how much she tried. 'Hey. How are you?'

He gave her a cheeky grin. 'Morning. Sorry, did I wake you?'

'No.' Abbie ran a hand over her hair and imagined how she must look with her plaits all out of control and fuzzy—and then decided that he'd have to take her or leave her. This was who she was. 'I've just been lazing around, y'know... D'you want to come in?'

Did she want him to? Hell, yes. But she wasn't sure it was such a good idea.

His eyes flitted down to her arm. 'In a minute. I just wanted to check you're okay. How's the wrist?'

It was throbbing as she hadn't taken her meds yet. She stretched it out a little, testing, twisting the cast back and forth. 'Sore. But okay. I won't be shooting clay things for a while.'

'Luckily, that's not what I had planned. I've

got something…' He looked a little abashed and for a moment she thought he was going to say something about yesterday, about the kiss. But he pointed over the balcony towards the car park. She stepped out into the surprisingly warm fresh air and looked down.

Whoa.

There was a Christmas tree roped onto the roof of his silver hatchback. The stump hung down to the car boot and was roped there too. 'Is that…is that for me?'

'The tree, not the car.' He laughed. 'You said you had a long list of things to do and, while I didn't know what else was on it, I did know this was. I thought you probably wouldn't be able to manage with your hand, so I got you one.'

It was huge; probably far too huge for her small apartment. A big bushy conifer, like something out of a magazine. It was such a thoughtful gesture it made her heart squeeze. 'It's lovely. Thank you.'

'And I have some decorations too. I didn't get many because I assumed you'd have some already, somewhere. If you want me to get them for you I can.' Cal paused. 'Did I do something wrong?'

There were tears pricking her eyes and she blinked them back. Because he was carving a way into her heart and she couldn't stop it. 'No. Not at all. It's really lovely.'

He looked relieved. 'I feel bad about the arm, to be honest. It's my fault you fell from the horse. I shouldn't have been acting the way I did.'

She thought about his brother and the way he was always so protective of him and realised that was his way. He saw himself as responsible for people, for making sure they didn't get hurt. 'Don't be silly. You didn't make me stand up in the saddle.'

'But I knew you would if I did.'

'I'm not that gullible.' But he was right, she'd been so competitive and determined to play that she hadn't given any thought to her own safety. Well, things were going to change. No more games. She would invite him in, thank him and then explain that the kiss had been the beginning and end of anything between them. Stepping back, she opened the door wide. 'You'd better come in.'

'Wait right there. I'll just grab the tree.'

And so he did. Then he went back down to get a box of baubles and tinsel and it was, *almost*, the nicest thing anyone had ever done for her. Because nothing could ever beat carrying a baby for you...but this was pretty special.

So she didn't have time to have a shower or anything except a face wash and teeth clean while he was at the car, and he didn't seem to mind that she was in her pyjamas—in fact, he'd looked at her clothes and grinned. Smiled, actually, a slow sexy smile that seemed to reach down into her gut and stroke it.

She pulled herself together. 'Right, well, I have a box in the top cupboard, just here, we'll just need to drag it out.'

'Okay. Lead on.'

'Just up there. At the back. Behind those boxes...yes, it says "XMAS" on it.' In the tiny hallway she watched the shift of his T-shirt across his taut stomach as he stretched, and the pull of his arm muscles as he dragged down the box with strands of red tinsel trailing down the side.

Since when had she found arm muscles attractive? Biceps brachii. Extensor carpi radialus longus. Abductor pollicis brevis. That was all they were. Not arms that had wrapped around her and pressed her against his chest. Or hands that had cupped her face and stroked her skin.

Just muscles. Nothing to get worked up about.

She hadn't even had time to tidy things up. But she looked at the place through his eyes—heck, he was a man, he wouldn't care that her huge red cushions weren't exactly straight, or that there were parenting magazines still open on the large window seat that looked up to the mountains.

Surely he'd gloss over the piles of baby things she'd left out, just so she could see them.

She loved the place; decorating it in the bright blues and greens had been part of her healing process. She'd wanted to cover the drab beige that reminded her of illness and disease with something vibrant and alive. It had given her and Emma something else to focus on for a while.

When Cal had brought the box through to the lounge and she'd managed to control her wayward feelings she flicked on the music system. 'I never, ever dress the tree without Christmas music, so hang on. Let me find a play list.'

He pulled a face. 'Oh, God, it's too early. Way too early. I should have offered to do some painting or DIY or something. Anything but death by "I Saw Mommy Kissing Santa Claus".'

'How dare you? This is the first time in years I've been excited about Christmas.' She flicked some tinsel towards him and it caught him under the chin. He chuckled. She laughed, and it felt so nice to be looking forward; her heart was fluttering a little at the anticipation of new beginnings. 'Don't you spoil it for me, Callum Baird.'

'I wouldn't dare.' His eyes widened as if he knew the kind of things she'd like to do to him. 'I know I can't outrun you, so I'm doomed.'

There was an ease with which they started to put things on the branches. As if they both instinctively knew where things should go; even the childish hand-painted baubles that Rosie had given her. But too soon they were reaching to the bottom of the box and the only ones left were the named ones Michael had bought in Sydney. Callum picked up the one with her husband's name on it and handed it to her. 'I think you should put this one on.'

'Thanks. Yes.' She put it where it always went: near the top of the tree, next to hers. It had been a fun anniversary weekend when they'd stumbled on a little market in Paddington. She'd been looking at a jewellery stall and he'd surprised her with these Christmas baubles. One each. Just one each. She'd been on pregnancy number two and they hadn't dared tell anyone as yet. They hadn't bought Bump a bauble, or done any baby shopping at all because they'd learnt the first time that putting all those things into tissue paper and into a box at the back of a cupboard was heartbreaking. By the time that Christmas came around they'd already started grieving for the second baby they'd lost.

In hindsight, they'd had a bad run of Christmases all round.

But for the first time in a long time she didn't well up at the thought of Michael missing another one. Sure, sadness still came in waves, but she knew now that no amount of wishing was going

to bring him back. She had to move on. She'd
never forget him, but she was going to make the
most of every day.

Cal was watching her as she hung the bauble
up.

'Are you okay?' he asked, his voice quiet and
concerned, but loud enough that she could still
hear him over someone dreaming of a white
Christmas. The lights twinkled on the tree and
she wondered if Michael was looking down from
somewhere and whether he was happy she'd
found Cal, even for a few weeks, or whether he'd
be disappointed, or sad. And then the tears did
threaten.

Make the most of every day.

'Yes. Surprisingly. I am. I'm fine. Thank you
for doing this. It's lovely.' Fine, but she didn't
want to dwell on things. She also wasn't sure
whether she wanted to walk into his arms to
hold him, one last time, and what kind of reaction she'd get if she did. So she held back, even
though every atom in her body was tugging towards him. 'What kind of Christmas will you
be having back home?'

He shrugged. 'Knowing Finn there'll be a lot
of booze; we usually go to our neighbours' house
for turkey and the trimmings. We've known
them all our lives.'

'What about your parents? Won't they be around?'

'Mam died a couple of years ago, just before the accident, thank God, because she'd have been so upset by that. She had a bad stroke and never recovered. Dad left us years before that. We don't see him. Don't even know where he is.'

'That's a shame.' So they had no family close to support them. No doubt that was why he took the job of looking after his brother so seriously. There wasn't anyone else to do it.

'It is how it is. Can't change things.' He reached deep into the bottom of the box and pulled out a rather bedraggled angel with bent wings, which he handed to her, because clearly he knew exactly where that was going. The very top. She took hold of it in her sore hand, forgetting that it was so bruised, and winced. 'Angel Gabrielle, yes, I know…' She cringed. 'I couldn't think of a better name when I was six. She has been passed down in the family since for ever. I will never ever have anything else on top of my tree.'

He held her good arm as she stood on a dining chair and placed Gabrielle on the top. 'Funny how everyone has their own traditions. We have a few silly ones too. Or did have—me and Finn can't be bothered these days.'

'Like what?'

'Ach, you know…putting coins in the pudding, dousing it in whisky and setting fire to it, you know…'

'You should keep those traditions going.' Easy for her to say when she'd avoided Christmas altogether for the last few years. 'Although, do be careful with the setting-fire thing. And do you really not cook at all?'

'No. Mam was the heart and soul of the village, so everyone's only too happy to make sure we don't starve and there's no end of invitations. You can't ever be lonely in Duncraggen, believe me.'

Abbie stepped down from the chair and there was a moment again where her body seemed magnetically attracted to his, and she was sure he was feeling the same because his eyes misted the second they touched. All he was doing was steadying her, but she needed a little more than a strong hand to shift her equilibrium back.

It was no good. It didn't matter how much she told herself to forget him, she just couldn't. She wanted to kiss him. And more. She wanted to… *calm down*. He was leaving—dammit; he was talking about the place he was going back to.

'It sounds lovely. I imagine Christmas in Scotland will be very snowy and magical, like something out of a film.'

'I suppose it is.' He was quiet for a moment.

'It's because of the people in the village that I'm here at all. They clubbed together and paid my fare and we made a roster of who was going to look after Finn while I wasn't there.'

She sensed they were heading into emotional territory and wouldn't have been surprised if he'd clammed up again, because that was his way. But she so wanted to know what had happened, to understand him, to help...possibly. She didn't even know why. Why did Callum have such an arrow straight to her heart?

Even though her fingers had hovered again and again over the keyboard, she hadn't looked him up. It was almost killing her, but she'd stayed true to her word. She wandered over to the window seat and sat down, trying to sound nonchalant and not too intrusive, while hoping he'd open up just a little. 'So the accident was two years ago? That's still very fresh, then.'

He came over and waited while she shovelled the parenting magazines onto the floor, then he sat next to her, leaning against the corner between the window and the wall. 'Aye. It's why I've made sure we have a SARS team now in the village and why I'm here to learn as much as I can and take it back to them.'

'So what did happen?'

'A blizzard, a white-out. We lost our bearings and he fell. It took them a while to find us.

The roads were all cut off and visibility was so bad they couldn't get the helicopters in. It was too risky for anyone to come find us at first. A total disaster.'

'So how long were you up there? What the hell were you doing all that time? Finn was injured? How badly?'

He shook his head, his eyes drifting to the mountain peak, still covered in snow. 'It doesn't matter.'

She shuffled forward. 'Actually, it does matter. It matters to me. It matters to Finn. And clearly it matters to you. Tell me?'

'Why? It only brings it all up. I don't talk about it. Full stop.'

He was retreating again, shutting down, and she didn't want him to. It wasn't good for him. Or her. 'So help me out a little. There are so many gaps in this story and I'm filling them with my own bleak thoughts.' She watched as he shook his head and turned away. 'It's okay. Honestly, I don't need to know. I understand you might not want to dredge all those things up again. But, even if you don't want to talk to me, you need to talk to him. Definitely you need to talk to Finn. One thing I learned with Michael was that we needed to communicate about how we were feeling. Otherwise you end up guessing. Guessing's no good. You need to know if someone needs your help getting through stuff, not be shut out.'

She thought he might recoil at the mention of Michael in amongst all of this, as if they were having a competition about who'd suffered the most, but he didn't.

'We're all different, Abbie. We don't all have to put our feelings out there to be stamped on. It's not my way.'

She pressed her good palm onto his hand. 'I know. But right now you can't even say the words. That can't be healthy, right?'

'But if I start I might not stop. If I don't even go there, I get to control what happens in here.' He tapped his head, then looked embarrassed at his outburst. He shrugged. 'It's difficult.'

'I didn't say it was going to be easy. But you'll be surprised how much it helps to give voice to those feelings—they do tend to float away for a bit.'

'I want them gone for good.'

'So make a start. You were on the Munro, right? It was snowing, you got lost.'

His eyes rolled as if he was being pressed into something he really didn't want to do, but knew he couldn't get out of it. Worse, actually, his tone was emotionless, as if he'd subsumed all feeling. She guessed it was the only way he dealt with this. 'Ben Arthur. The mountain. It's usually not too difficult in the summer. But we thought we'd have a challenge and go up in January. It's a scramble at the top, challenging, but anyone can do it with a bit of care.'

He stared out of the window, his features hollowed out somehow as he retreated into his memories. 'Going down's always the tricky bit. You know? I mean, the uphill always hurts the most, but, when you're tired after all the exertion, it's the going down that can be the most dangerous. We were pretty high, though. We'd got up in record time; it had been an easy stroll. We were chatting about what we were going to do that evening to celebrate when it suddenly started to snow. Not little wisps, I mean huge flakes, thick and fast, that were sticking to the ground. So we upped our pace. Nothing to worry about. But after a few minutes we couldn't see anything around us; we were *in* the snow cloud. It was freezing and it was like we were walking blind. We couldn't see our outstretched hands, never mind the path, and we must have wandered off somehow. It's easy to get disoriented in those conditions.'

'Yes. It's scary too.' She gave words to the feelings she thought he might have, hoping that to name them would help him acknowledge them. They were easier to let go that way.

'We argued over which way to go. He wouldn't

listen to me. I wouldn't listen to him. Things got pretty ugly.'

He sucked in a deep breath and she didn't know how to respond to any of this so she just let him go on. 'I insisted we should go one way. He disagreed, told me I always thought I was right... I pulled at him to listen, there was a bit of rough. Brother stuff. Nothing and everything; panic rolled into sibling rivalry and then some. Then the next thing, he disappeared. Just disappeared in front of my eyes.'

'God, that's horrific. I can't imagine.'

'There was a steep drop, a sheer cliff, and he just fell over it. I mean, how could that happen?' He shook his head. 'I didn't mean to...'

'To what?' Her heart was thundering now.

He didn't answer her. 'I could just about make him out at the bottom, motionless, I didn't know what the hell to do. All my training just faded from my head and I just shouted. Like an idiot. I'm shouting into the air for someone to come and help us. To save us.'

At least with Michael they'd had help, so much help. They'd been frightened, but there had been no end of assistance and advice and love. Being alone on a mountain and unable to do anything must have been desperate.

His voice was still completely flat. 'You know the rest. The snow, the delay. I managed to climb down to him using some rope we'd taken with us to do some rock-climbing practice before we started the hike. And he was just…cold. So cold.'

'I can't imagine how you must have felt, what you thought.'

'He was so badly broken I thought he was going to die. I made my peace with him. I promised him that if he held on then I'd do everything to help him get better. He kept his side of the bargain and I kept mine.'

'I'd say you did more than that.'

'Hell, yes. He should never have gone over in the first place.'

There was something in his tone that she didn't understand. 'You're saying that was your fault?'

Cal looked broken, bleak. 'I'm saying that if we hadn't tussled and I hadn't been so cocksure which way we were heading, he'd still have two damn legs. Yes.'

'You can't possibly put blame on anyone. It was an accident.'

'That could have been avoided. I, more than anyone, know that.'

He needed to understand—believe—that there was either no blame, or equal blame. 'He walked up that hill just the same as you did. Don't tell me he doesn't feel responsible too.'

'I shouldn't have suggested we took that route.'

'It was dark, snowing. You couldn't see. Who

knows what might have happened if you'd just stayed where you were. You could have died of hypothermia.'

He shook his head. 'He might have two working legs.'

'And he might be dead. So might you.'

They sat in silence for a while as they both went over the events of that night. It had scarred him very deeply, and clearly he wore that responsibility like a brand.

'So you gave up your job to look after him? Moved back home?'

'Aye. I was going places in Edinburgh, you know, in the ambulance service. Promotion, awards... But I'm okay with going back to Duncraggen. Really. It's a lot smaller, but I love being a paramedic and I can give so much back to the community that saved us...that saved Finn's life.'

But he took that responsibility very seriously now, that was clear; he'd given up his career to care for his brother.

There were a few more moments of quiet and she waited for him to say more. He didn't. He just stared out of the window at the mountains, and her heart contracted a little. Because she knew how he was feeling—that he was trying to make sense of something and he couldn't.

Because life happened and sometimes it was amazing and sometimes it broke your heart into tiny little pieces and you just couldn't put them back together again. She imagined him up there making all those promises to his brother, to himself, staring death right in the face. Wishing he'd made better decisions. Wishing it had been him who had fallen. And her heart started to break a little more.

She reached out to his arm, stroking and stroking, and after a while his shoulders relaxed and he breathed deeply. After a few moments he covered her hand with his and looked at her, smiling and shrugging off the emotion and the memories.

He sat forward and reached out to her hair, ran a stray lock of it through his fingers. 'So that's the tale of the infamous Baird Boys.'

'Thank you for letting me in.' She found him a smile. 'Feel better?'

'I don't know.' As he let the lock of hair drop he glanced down at her legs that she'd pulled up onto the seat cushion. His fingers trailed over her ankle, drawing tiny circles in the little dimple on the inside of her foot. She knew she should have pulled away, but it was so delicious to have his hands on her again. To feel the sadness evaporate and to see his gaze change from haunted to heated. To know that she did that to him.

She knew, oh, she knew a zillion things, but she didn't say a word about any of them, or about the decisions she'd made about calling a halt to all this.

When he leaned in and tilted her chin up she let him.

And when he slid his mouth over hers she let him—no, she encouraged him. She wrapped her arms around his neck and pulled him close so she could feel the beat of his heart against hers, so she could breathe him in and feel his heat. So she could tell him with her body and her sighs that she wanted him, that he wasn't to blame, he'd saved his brother's life. Because, hell…she wanted him to kiss her, to make love to her, to hold her into the night.

One thing she'd learned was that there were few moments in life that were truly beautiful, and this was one of them. This was one that she didn't want to let go, one she didn't want to forget. So she kissed him back, hard and deep until she didn't just want him inside her, she needed him there.

When he pulled away he was breathless, his eyes glittering with more than just desire. 'Abbie, tell me to stop if you don't want this.'

'I don't want you to stop, Cal. I know it's crazy. We shouldn't do anything more, because I know this can't go anywhere, but I can't stop.'

'You and me both.' His fingers ran down the

opening of her dressing gown. 'Tell me the truth, lassie. I woke you up, didn't I?'

'Yes. Yes, you did.'

'So, you want to go back to bed, aye?'

She'd never been outright asked before, not like that. Heat pooled low in her gut. 'Yes.'

'Good. Because I want to take you to bed and kiss every inch of you.' He gave her a wry smile by way of explanation and the mood got lighter. 'You did say I should voice my feelings.'

'You're talking about sex, not feelings.' Sex. Yes. Sex was good. Simple. Animal. Natural. Sex.

And now it was her turn not to want to acknowledge the emotions swirling around her chest.

His forehead was against hers. 'You want me to lay my heart out for you, do you?'

'Yes. No. I don't know. It's so hard, Cal. One minute I think I know what I want, then I get confused.' She didn't want to lay her heart out to him the way he just had to her; to admit there was a raw heat under her ribcage and it was all mixed up with images of him desperately trying to save his brother. Of his kisses that were so consuming. Of the thought of him getting on a plane and never coming back.

'Okay, Abbie. Let me tell you what *I* want.' He pressed a kiss to the dip at the base of her throat, making her shudder with desire. 'I want you like I've never wanted anyone before.'

Another kiss to her collarbone, a trail of little presses to her shoulder. 'I want to peel these clothes off you. I want to take you to bed and watch you come. I want to hear you sigh. I want to kiss you from head to toe. I want to be inside you, hell…more than that. So much more.' He closed his eyes and swallowed. When he opened them again they were burning with heat. Over the top of her robe he palmed her breast, his breathing ragged. '*Just* sex is something different altogether.'

And so what did all this mean? Was he hers to take and have and then give up?

The thought of him leaving made her gut curl and her head hurt. The thought of keeping him here, just for now, was so overwhelming, so delicious she couldn't contemplate any other outcome. She pressed her palm against his chest, felt the strong, fast beat of his heart, ran her fingers up to his neck, his jaw, tried to make light of something that was very, very momentous indeed. 'I will, if you will.'

'No more games, Abbie. Not this time. This time we both get to win.' He took hold of her broken wrist and kissed along her knuckles so gently it made her heart contract.

'Yes. Yes.' She'd never felt more certain about

anything in her life. She wanted him and she wasn't going to let anything get in the way of that. Because tomorrow, later, for the rest of her life she would be Abbie the mum, Abbie the widow, Abbie the nurse, Abbie the friend...

'In that case, what are we waiting for?' Cal's beautiful blue eyes danced over her fingers as he sucked one gently into his mouth. The sensation of his hot wet tongue on her skin sent her body into overdrive. Her eyes connected with his and the connection between them seemed to tug tighter and tighter.

She was going to bed with him.

He smiled a wicked smile, that stoked more heat in her belly, and looked back down at her hand.

And she saw the exact moment doubt clouded his head.

He went completely still, focusing on her wedding ring. 'Actually, no. We've both made promises to other people. We'll stop right now.'

CHAPTER TEN

WHAT THE HELL had they been thinking?

There was her wedding ring glinting in the Christmas tree light and, no matter what, he couldn't make love to another man's wife. She had so many things going on in her life, getting involved with a man who was duty bound to go halfway across the world would only muddle all that. He couldn't take on the responsibility for her happiness or heartbreak too.

Cal tugged away from her, letting her hand go, gently—because she was still hurting.

And, dammit, he was hurting her even more by pushing her away, but it was for her own good. 'I can't, Abbie. *We* can't.'

She looked down at her ring and pressed her lips tight together, eyes now shimmering with the sheen of tears. She shook her head. And again.

And his heart just about melted. 'I understand, Abbie, it's okay. You loved him. And I'm not...' *Him.* He had no words. He wasn't about to cuckold a memory for the sake of a roll in bed. And yes, he knew his feelings were more than that; that somehow he'd become all tangled up with this woman. But there was a line he wasn't prepared to step over no matter how much his body begged him to. She was wearing Michael's ring. She was still in love with his memory. 'We can't.'

She touched his arm, breathing out long and slow. 'Yes. We can. I can. It's time, Cal. I've been putting it off for too long and I should have done it a long time ago.'

'Not on my account. I don't want you to do anything like that for my sake.'

'This isn't about you, it's about me. About letting go of the past and moving forward—we both know we have to do some of that, right?' She tugged off her wedding ring—more difficult, given her swollen wrist—felt the weight of the gold in her hand. And he saw in it all the promises she'd made to her husband.

Short of begging his brother not to die, this was the most intimate thing he'd ever done. And he wasn't sure if he could handle it. Yet even so, far from this being a killer of his desire, it only made the ties to her feel stronger. Because of all the men in the whole damned world she could have done this with, she'd chosen him. There was a hitch in his chest, something shifting, making space. It felt blown wide open and yet also crushed tight.

'Can you unfasten my necklace for me?' She gave him a wobbly smile and he could see she was holding back more tears.

He frowned. 'No. Not for me, don't do this for me.' It was too much to ask of him, too much responsibility.

'It's for me. Help me, please, Cal. I want to kiss you again. I want to go to bed with you.' Now she laughed, a little. Decision made. She looked as if she believed the words she was saying. 'Don't make me beg.'

'I wouldn't dare.' He was all thumbs as he turned her away from him and gripped the fragile chain, eventually releasing the thin gold clasp, then after he'd handed it to her she slid the ring onto the chain and he fastened it back around her neck.

She turned, fingering the ring for a moment then letting it drop to hang loose at her throat. Her eyes glistened as she looked up at him. 'To be absolutely honest with you, I don't really know if I am ready. I don't know if this is going to be the best decision I've ever made or the worst one, and I certainly don't know what the hell is going to happen to us in ten minutes, never mind tomorrow or next week. But I've spent years avoiding hurt by not getting close to anyone. Now I'm scared about how much I'll hurt if I don't. All I can think about is that I want you. So badly.'

That was some huge admission, but she was right. He hadn't wanted to get close to her either, but trying to pretend it wasn't happening wasn't getting them anywhere. He reached for her and pulled her close, wrapping his arms around her, because he couldn't stop this. Couldn't fight the stirring in his belly and the overwhelming need for her that came from nowhere. He couldn't fight it, didn't want to, not today. Not in this moment.

'Come here.'

She slid her arms around his waist and laid her head against his chest and they stood, locked together, not fighting, not playing, not racing. Just feeling the beat of their two hearts as they mingled into one steady rhythm, and still listening to the Christmas music that was now harking on about it being cold outside.

Actually, the sun was shining on a late spring day, but it was no match for the heat in here. Because, regardless of all his principles, he was still very hot for a gorgeous woman in a silk robe. Hot for *this* woman, who was a combination of all things sexy and funny, kind and sincere and yet a fighter. A survivor. The whole package. Perfect.

Whoa.

Perfect was a lot to get his head around.

'You okay?' she asked him. 'I haven't frightened you off?'

'I'm good.' But his heart started to hammer and he had to admit to being spooked. If she was perfect, that meant he might just fall for her. Completely.

Maybe he already had. Too hard. Too quick. But even though all logic told him to leave right now and get his head straight, his feet were stuck to the floor, his arms locked around her.

He felt her smile against his chest. 'Me too. I'm very, very good.'

'And, I've finally found a way to keep you still,' he whispered into her ear, rubbing his cheek against her head, breathing her in.

'We'll see about that.' She wriggled away from him, tipping her head back and laughing. 'Race you to the bedroom.'

'But—' This wasn't how he did things—leaping from intensity to humour, from comfort to need. He usually did the slow build, or hot and raw, not zigzagging from one to the other and everything in between. Or maybe it was how he did things now. Maybe this was his new normal; experiencing the whole range of emotions in as many minutes. Maybe this was what *she* did to him and would continue to do to him until he left. 'What about…?'

'It's this way…' There was a sparkle in her

eyes as she ran back to him and pressed her mouth to his. 'Surely, Callum Baird, you're not going to let me get there first?'

'Never.' Cal's arms snaked round her waist and he picked her up, scooping her legs into his arms as if she didn't weigh any more than a feather. Abbie hadn't got a clue what all this meant, why taking her ring off had felt like the right thing to do. All she knew was that there had been no way she could let Cal walk out of that door. There was a wave of guilt but she tried to convince herself that Michael would be happy for her. He would.

The atmosphere was changing lightning fast from intense to fun and she was struggling to catch up. It felt as if they were trying to make up for all the hours, weeks, years they hadn't known each other, trying to fit a lifetime into these moments. It was breathtaking, scary, exhilarating and tilting her a little off balance. When it came to Callum Baird she felt so many things. Too many.

He smiled and she felt that ping in her heart. 'If I carry you through we'll get there together,' he growled.

'Seriously, I can manage to walk.' She made a play of struggling, but in all truth it was divine to be in his arms. She leaned her head against his chest and breathed in his spicy scent, felt the bristles on his jaw scrape her forehead, felt the muscles on his arms contract and stretch, and everything tightened in anticipation of another kiss, of how he'd feel inside her.

He shook his head. 'Knowing you, you'll be racing to get undressed and in bed before I get the chance to take those clothes off your body. But believe me, lady—*I* am taking those clothes off.'

She pretended to weigh up her options, when the only reply was *how quickly*? 'Only if that means I get to undress you too.'

'I think we can manage that.' He laid her on the unmade bed and climbed in next to her, looking at her as if she'd saved his life, as if she'd hauled him off that mountain herself. 'But first, thank you. For being right there and listening.'

'Anyone would have listened, Cal.'

'No one would have known how right it was to say it out loud, no one would have pushed so gently, yet so perfectly. But you did, Abbie. You did.' He leaned over, cupped her face in his hands and angled his mouth over hers in a bone-melting intimate kiss born of all the emotions they'd just shared. It was a caress, a promise of no more hurt, a wiping away of pain. It was the seal of something—a connection so raw and genuine and pure that she thought her heart was going to burst open. She needed him and, miracle of miracles, he needed her right back.

But when he groaned into her mouth the kiss turned feverish, kindling hot need inside her, spreading fast through her body. It deepened into seeking out his tongue, clashing teeth, a biting-lips kind of kiss.

Dragging her mouth from his for the short-est second she could bear, she tugged at his T-shirt, pulling it over his head and throwing it aside. Ran her hands over finely sculpted mus-cles, sighing in pleasure at this beautiful man, ignoring the wrist twinges and the heartache and the knowledge that this could only be temporary, fleeting—because nothing was going to stop her exploring every inch of him.

As she kissed across his chest, from one nip-ple to the other, making him laugh, his fingers tore at her robe, then her pyjama top and he was groaning again as he looked at her, half naked and all turned on. 'God, Abbie, you drive me mad.'

'I hope that's a good thing.' She straddled him, pressing fast kisses to his throat as his hands palmed her breasts, shuddering as he sat up and caught her nipples in his mouth. Beneath her bottom she could feel how much he wanted her and she writhed against his erection, desperate to be relieved of her shorts and him his jeans.

She arched her back as he sucked her nipple, intensifying her need to fever pitch.

'Aye, it's a very good thing.' He flipped her onto her back and ground against her, breathless, his hand now stroking the tender part of her hip. She reached down and unzipped his jeans and he wriggled out of them, then discarded them on the floor. He, in turn, stripped her of her shorts and within seconds they were both naked.

Somehow he was standing next to the bed and she was lying on the duvet, momentarily transfixed by his body. He was...*oh*, he was impressive. Her mouth dried just looking at the rock-hard abs and the trail of fine hair down, down, down... He was divine. She knelt up and reached for his hips, tugging him towards her, taking his erection in her good hand, her mouth inches from the tip. But at her touch he sucked in air, covering her hand with his own, cursing and laughing.

'Abbie, if this was a race, I'd definitely be losing right now. So give me a fighting chance, won't you?'

Then he pushed her back onto the bed and his mouth was on her thigh and his hands under her bottom, his stubble grazing her skin, and it felt amazing. A sweet pleasure and pain, which she never wanted to stop.

For a fleeting moment she wondered how it

would be, with him. Whether she'd please him. Whether she'd be enough for Cal. Because she hadn't done this for such a long time…

But Callum's fingers pressed against her core and all thought shut off. Then his mouth found her centre and the wet heat on her thighs and his rhythmic kisses hypnotised her, drugged her, completely took over her brain and her body.

She felt her release rising and bucked against his mouth, hanging on, hanging on… 'Cal, Cal! I need you inside me.'

'Soon. Soon. Not yet.'

But just as she thought she couldn't hold on any more, he pulled away. And smiled.

For one cold second she wondered what he was doing, then she understood.

Condom.

She could have told him it wasn't necessary. She wanted to shout out, she wanted him inside her. *Now.* Nothing else mattered, the world could wait. Only he mattered. Them. This.

But then he was over her, pushing gently…so gently, too gently, so she raised her hips to meet him and he filled her, stripping her breath on a moan. She felt her core contract as he began to move inside her, his kisses greedy. Hungry. She tried to hang onto a single thread of control, but with Cal all control was lost.

It was scary and yet wonderful. Something

she'd never thought she'd experience again; to meet someone, to do this.

His gaze connected with hers, his fingers entwined with hers, his body moved in time with hers as if they were two halves of one whole. Harder. Faster. Her release started to build, more intensely now, as she met him thrust for thrust. Then he rocked hard against her, moaning into her hair, her name on his lips over and over and she tightened around him. He was crying out and she with him, both racing to the edge. Both winning.

She couldn't let him go. As the high began to recede she pulled him back to look at her, covering his face in kisses that came straight from her heart. And he stroked her hair, surely a derailed mess by now, and he smiled his heart-melting smile. 'Well, I think I'd call that a draw, wee lass.'

'Yes. That was definitely a win-win.' But as she looked deep into those bluest eyes, at that beautiful face, as she breathed him in and wrapped him close, her heart squeezed so viciously at the thought of him leaving.

And she knew...

She was irrevocably lost.

It took Callum some time to find his equilibrium—actually, he doubted he'd ever find it properly again while he was under Abbie's spell. He rolled onto his back, dragging in ragged breaths, and she wrapped herself into his arms, her legs lazily draped over his.

Meanwhile, he felt the furthest from lazy. His heart was thudding along at a rapid pace and his brain was whirling with a whole load of questions. How could it be possible to feel so connected with someone when logic told you it was a stupid idea? How could she have taken possession of his heart so quickly?

He wanted to move, to be alone with his thoughts and work out what the best thing to do would be for both of them, but didn't want to disturb her. She looked so comfortable, so thoroughly satisfied; as if nothing was troubling her at all.

Maybe when he left here today, she'd slip from his mind. Maybe he'd forget her the moment he got on the plane.

Yeah, that was just wishful thinking. Reality was, he'd never forget her. She was bruised on his heart now.

She sighed and for a moment he thought she was falling asleep, but then she spoke. 'I wish you weren't going back to Scotland. I know it's immensely selfish of me, but I really do wish you were here for a bit longer.'

Her honesty hit him hard in the solar plexus.

She put words to the feelings he had and tried to hide from himself. 'Yes. But I've got to go home. There is no debate there.'

'For your Scottish Christmas.'

'For my job, my brother. My life. I just happen to be going back in time for Christmas.' Today had been the closest he'd be getting to the best of Christmas cheer, he reckoned. He couldn't remember a time when putting up a Christmas tree had made him feel so much.

'Do you have a going-home date?'

'My ticket's booked and paid for. I leave on the eighteenth.'

'So soon?' She wound her legs around his calves and tugged herself closer, and he kissed the top of her head, breathing her in and trying to commit her scent to memory.

She had so much to look forward to, she'd easily forget he'd ever been here. Even her house pulsed with the anticipation of the baby and a future; bags brimming with tiny clothes, nappies, toys in the corner of the lounge. She was moving forward while he was going back. 'Ach, you'll have the baby soon and I'll just be the guy who bridged the waiting time until you got your family. You won't miss me.'

'Oh, I will.' With a sad smile she squeezed against him and he caught the scent of her again.

It felt as if it were part of him now. 'What do you do for him? For Finn?'

Cal sat up at the mention of his brother's name and the reality of what they faced. 'He's had a difficult recovery. Complicated. There was the frostbite, lower leg amputation, broken pelvis. Dislocated shoulder. Displaced collarbone. Minor head injury. He couldn't drive for a long time so I took him back and forth to appointments. He had a lot of adjusting to do. A hell of a lot. He's a physiotherapist, so he had some understanding of what's required, but he's so damned impulsive and impatient. And he loved playing rugby—any sport, really. So his whole life has changed. He was down for a long time.'

'By down, do you mean depressed?'

He kept looking straight ahead because to see her soft eyes would make him give in to the emotion he kept firmly locked inside. 'Aye. I had to keep watch…you know. A few times. I was worried he might…well, finish the job off altogether.'

He'd almost lost his brother over and over. Unable to do anything but watch as drink had almost pushed him over the edge. As darkness had shrouded him too many times. Abbie hitched herself up next to him and stroked her fingers down his cheek, pressed a kiss there.

'That would have been so hard on you. Did he get help?'

'In the end, yes. He did. Don't get me wrong, he's a natural optimist, but he was badly broken in body and spirit. It took some working out in his head to try to get better. But he still struggles with sleep and some pain, and yet with planning a ski trip and more climbing I get the impression he thinks he's bloody Superman.'

She laughed and prodded his shoulder. 'Don't all men?'

And now it was time to put all that darkness aside, and relish these fleeting moments. He dug deep and found her a smile, flexing his biceps. 'I don't *think* I'm Superman, I know I am.'

'God, yes.' She straddled him again, and his body reacted exactly as it always did when she was around. And for the next few minutes he showed her just exactly what he meant.

Afterwards, he brought coffee through to the bedroom and he could see by the dancing in her eyes that she was brewing an idea and her body was restless. He gave her a cup and perched on the bed next to her. 'Ants in yer pants again?'

She grinned. 'I feel like I need to get out in the fresh air. Come for a walk with me?'

'Are you sure that's a good idea with your injured hand?'

'I use my feet to walk. I'll be fine.' She put out her hand and rotated her wrist, clearly trying to mask the grimace. 'It's fine.'

'It still hurts.'

'Of course it does. I can't use it properly, but if I just sit here ruminating I'll focus on the pain. If I get outdoors I can focus on other things.' She ran her good fingers over his chest. 'Or... I can think of other things to focus on too.'

There was nothing more he wanted than to stay here in bed, but every kiss, every stroke chipped away at his resolve and his heart. 'Give a man a chance to recover.'

'Oh? What's happened to Superman all of a sudden?'

'He needs some down time. Literally.' Something purely physical, rather than emotional, might help his heart and head settle down a little. Now he understood why she kept on moving; it meant she didn't have to dwell on what was really going on. 'Okay, a walk sounds good. The lake path again?'

She shook her head. 'There are plenty of lovely walks around here. We can stop off and get a packed lunch and then decide.'

It was only just past midday, but it felt like a lifetime ago that he'd turned up here with the tree. He looked down at his clothes strewn over the floor. 'Okay, swing by my place and let me find some decent walking clothes.'

She looked at him over the steam from her mug. 'Yes, oh, and I mustn't forget to feed Eric's cats.'

'And pick up Rosie? The play park?'

'Not today. Emma's picking her up after her shift, but I do have to be back in reasonable time because I promised them we'd put the cot together tonight.'

For some reason this simple statement made Cal's chest hurt. He imagined the two women screwing bits of wood together to make a whole lot more than a bed—it was a life. A life so full she definitely wouldn't miss him. He almost offered to help, then realised he'd be butting in on something very intimate, something that didn't involve him.

So what kind of idiot would willingly walk this path when the reality was staring him in the face? There could be no future here; he could not stay. His responsibilities were to his brother, the village, another life.

Finn would laugh and tell him to enjoy the ride. But when the ride became so addictive that you didn't want to get off, what did you do?

Finn. The thought of his brother and the accident gave Callum pause. He was trying to hang onto his emotions, but he felt as if he were watching himself go over the cliff. Like his brother, he was falling too hard and too fast and there was only one guarantee—he would hurt like hell when he landed.

CHAPTER ELEVEN

'IF I DIDN'T know any better I'd think you were taking me up Ben Lomond.'

'I thought we could do just go up in the gondola, maybe have a coffee and see how we feel.' Yes, she was going to take him up Ben Lomond, because why the heck not? She liked the walk and he would too, if he ever gave her a chance. Although, she noticed his voice had an edge to it and she wasn't entirely sure if she should push him.

Abbie told him to pull the car into the gondola car park and tried to pretend everything was fine. It wasn't. Something had happened during their lovemaking that had made her feel so totally connected to him and utterly bereft at him leaving.

In her roundabout way, she'd asked him to stay and he'd again pointed out all the reasons he couldn't. So now she wanted to exercise off the weird feelings running through her. She needed to protect herself and her heart from falling in love with him. That couldn't happen.

So, not spending any more time with him would have been the best approach, but there was one thing she wanted to do, for him…and she didn't want to think about anything past that. 'It's a lovely day, and there are wonderful views. And the gondola ride's always fun. Hey, we could luge our way down.'

'Or we could just luge all day and not go up the mountain.' He grinned, although she could see the guarding in his eyes. He'd gone from being honest and open to closed off. 'Be honest, Abbie, you're pushing me again. I told you I didn't want to do this with you. You know what I think about it.'

She tucked her arm into his and smiled innocently. 'Oh, come on, it's a lovely day and we won't go all the way to the top. Trust me.'

He let out a heavy sigh. 'It's not you I have a problem with.'

The gondola swung precariously in the wind as it inched up the mountain. It was a spectacular day of sunshine but there was still quite a breeze. In the big metal and glass cabin with them was a heavily pregnant woman and her husband. Abbie smiled. 'When are you due?'

'January.' The woman ran her hand over her belly, but even though she looked thrilled at her condition she didn't look particularly enamoured with the ride. Every time the wind blew she grabbed hold of her husband's fist. 'This is our babymoon. We've come down from Nelson for a few days. I wanted some down time before the chaos hits.'

'First one?'

She beamed. 'Yes. I'm so excited. It's our miracle baby, you see. We tried so hard for so long and now here I am. I never thought I'd hit forty-one and then get pregnant. To be honest, I'm a bit nervous about it all.'

'Yes, I can imagine you would be. I'm sure it'll be wonderful.' Now was the time Abbie should have mentioned her own impending parenthood, but it would be too hard to explain. And she felt guilty that she was up here having a trip out when Emma was working.

But she was due to go on leave at the end of the week, so Abbie would make a double fuss of her then. Instead, she pointed out the sights to the holidaymakers.

As if reading her mind, Cal squeezed her hand and she squeezed back, glad that, even though they hadn't discussed what was next for them, he still wanted to stay physically close at least.

'Does it always swing like this?' The woman stared out of the window, her hand moving from her belly to her mouth. 'It makes me feel a bit sick.'

It hardly appeared to be moving at all now to Abbie. 'We're nearly at the top. The fresh air will help you. Take a few deep breaths when you get off. I'm sure you'll feel better.'

But the woman still looked green a little later after Abbie and Cal had had their coffee overlooking the town. And her ankles were suspiciously swollen under her maxi dress. She was sitting in the café with her head in her hands. Her husband was telling her she'd be fine and that she just needed to rest.

Abbie's nursing instinct made her stop and check. *Just in case,* she told Cal. 'Hi there, are you still not feeling great?'

'I'm just a bit dizzy and out of breath, that's all.' The woman grimaced, red-faced, but Abbie didn't think that was just from embarrassment.

'She's just been sick. I told her to try and eat something, but she doesn't want to.' The partner grimaced. 'The minute she feels well enough, we're heading back down and I'm going to make her go straight to bed.'

'Good idea. Maybe a quick trip to the doctor's en route.' Abbie smiled, knowing her face was a mask of friendliness, meanwhile assessing for any obvious signs and symptoms. 'Your husband is probably right—some rest would be good.'

Cal was also clearly a little concerned if his frown was anything to go by. 'Headache?'

The woman nodded. 'I've had it for a few days and I can't seem to get rid of it. I thought the fresh air would do me some good.'

Pre-eclampsia. All well and good to deal with in a hospital setting, but not so great at the top of a huge hill with only a swinging box to get them back down again. 'And the swelling in your feet, is that normal for you?'

The woman looked down at her shoes. 'No. It's not. But then, I've never been pregnant before so I don't know what normal is. I just thought that's what happened. You get fat all over, right?'

'Hey, well sometimes. My name is Abbie and I'm a nurse. Cal here is a paramedic. Is it okay if we sit with you for a while? Just to keep an eye on you until you feel better?' Cutting short the walk was nothing compared to making sure she was okay.

Cal nodded and joined them at the table, his voice gentle but probing. He'd gone straight into professional mode and Abbie was glad there was something to buffer the weird atmosphere between them. Only, she wished it weren't this: a potential emergency. 'What's your name?'

'Ashley. And thank you, you don't need to go to all this trouble. This is Mark, my partner.'

Cal patted her arm. 'It's no trouble. I was just

wondering, when did you last see a midwife or obstetrician?'

'Oh, a few weeks ago. I should have gone last week, but I was too busy at work. Then we came here and I've been trying to relax, but I do feel a little strung out.'

Alarm bells started ringing. She could have dangerously high blood pressure, be at risk of seizures and even a stroke. Death. The baby was at risk too. Abbie wasn't going to panic her, but she'd have felt better dealing with her in the ED. At least she'd have the equipment there; here she had nothing except her observation skills. 'I think it's probably a good idea to just get yourself checked out when you get down to town. No harm in checking, right?'

'Sur...' But the woman's words didn't come out properly and she started to slump to the side, into Cal's lap. He caught her and helped her back in the chair. 'Ashley? Ashley? Hey, we should stop meeting like this.'

Back to his black humour and Abbie loved him for it because it got a smile from both of the expectant parents. Although, Ashley's was pretty weak.

Mark grabbed Ashley's hand. 'Hey, girl. Hey. What's happening?' Then he looked over to Abbie, his voice rising. 'What's happening?'

'I'm not one hundred per cent sure, but she

may have pre-eclampsia, or just be dehydrated.' Or a dozen things that they couldn't deal with up here. *Please don't start fitting. Please, just don't.* 'We need to get her down to the ED as quickly as possible.' Trying not to look panicked, Abbie glanced over to Cal.

'I'm going to call my mates and get them to bring some reinforcements.' Cal fished his phone out of his pocket. 'There's a helicopter landing pad just outside. It shouldn't take them long to get here.'

But in the meantime there was little they could do apart from make her comfortable. Abbie moved her chair to be closer, stroked Ashley's hand and smiled. 'Got any names chosen yet?'

'Jessica Rose,' Mark answered when his girl-friend didn't seem to be able to make the words she was clearly trying to find come out of her mouth.

'Pretty. You know it's a girl, then?'

'Yes. Can't wait to meet her.'

'Not…yet…too…early.' Ashley was groggy and suddenly inhaled sharply, her head jerking back.

'She's having a seizure.' Abbie's heart started to beat rapidly. *No. No. No. No.* This couldn't happen.

Abbie sent Mark to ask for some space to be cordoned off and for blankets, and to make a makeshift bed on the floor. She rolled Ashley onto her side to protect her airway and held her head gently in a safe position. Time for mum and bub was starting to run out.

Meanwhile Cal had run outside at the sound of the chopper blades and was now reappearing with two of his colleagues.

'I have never been so glad to see you,' she whispered. Would she ever get sick of seeing that beautiful face? Of breathing him in? Right now she wanted to be in his arms in bed and not here facing this. She made it her priority not to get involved with men or patients, and yet here she was doing exactly that. She could barely breathe for worry about Ashley and that precious baby. And could barely look at Cal without the tug of desire and need.

Within minutes, Ashley was in the helo with Mark and it was lifting from the ground, but keeping as low as it could carrying a patient with dangerously high blood pressure. The magnesium sulphate had been administered to manage the fitting and she'd been given something to sedate her.

So, as they waved them off, Abbie should have been feeling more positive. She wasn't. She felt an overwhelming sense of dread.

Cal's arm was loosely wrapped around her shoulder. 'Hey, are you okay, Abbie?'

No. She wanted to lean against his chest and tell him about her fears. That the baby might not survive, and neither might Ashley. That she felt bad about being here, fit and well and not pregnant. For the first time ever, she was glad she wasn't pregnant and that made her feel very strange indeed.

She wanted to admit she was lonely and that he was the best thing that had happened to her in a very long time and that she didn't want him to leave. But couldn't ask him to stay either.

What man wanted to take on a woman and a baby and an almost co-dependent friendship set-up? Especially if that man had other reasons to go back to Scotland. Good, honourable reasons that she had no argument with.

'More, now than ever, I need to get rid of the adrenalin. I need to walk. Or run.' Or sex. Yes, sex would definitely bring her blood pressure right down. But she dragged on her backpack as best she could with one hand in a cast. 'Come on, let's get going before it gets too late.'

She started to hike, hard and fast, trying to put distance between them, concentrating on putting one foot in front of the other for as long and as fast as she could. Trying to wipe away the images of him in her bed and the hurt in her heart.

Soon her heart began pounding with the exercise and her head began to clear as the endorphins kicked in and she thought less and less about all the things pressing into her brain and more about just breathing.

After a good hour of pushing up and up and up through tussock grass and along thin gravel paths edged by tiny alpine plants, she heard his voice behind her. 'Abbie! Abbie, stop. For God's sake. Stop.'

She dropped her bag to the floor and grabbed a drink bottle from the side pocket, waiting for him to catch up. 'What's wrong? Can't keep up?'

'I just wanted to stop and admire the view. You know…smell the roses…instead of marching up to the top of the hill and marching down again.'

'Oh. Yes, of course.' That had been the reason to bring him in the first place—to show him how lovely it could be instead of worrying about danger and disaster and search and rescue. And his brother. 'Stunning, yes? And no issues, you see? Neither of us have fallen over or off and it hasn't snowed. We're not lost—the path is pretty easy to follow. We're fine. We're absolutely fine.'

They weren't fine, she knew that. But neither of them was prepared to talk about it. His eyebrows rose. 'I suppose.'

'How do you feel?'

He took a long deep breath and looked over the panoramic view of mountains and valleys and the bluest of blue lakes. His hair was tousled in the breeze and there wasn't a drip of sweat on him. It was as if he'd just gone for a stroll instead of scaling a peak. 'Great. Pretty damned good.'

'It's always good to face your demons.'

'Ach, how can I not when you're around?' He winked and then looked across the exposed terrain. Wind sliced through them and the grass bowed and swayed in one direction and then another. 'I admit, I was playing it cautious, but I'm learning. Live and let live. Give support and don't overpower. Right?'

'Right. And learn to trust in other people's ideas and dreams.'

'It's harder than you think.' He tilted her chin so he could look at her. 'But thanks for that, Abbie.'

'Oh, you're absolutely welcome. But who am I to give advice? I don't have any kids... yet.' She couldn't help but press her good palm to his cheek. It was cold from the fresh southerly breeze, but his eyes were warm and she stood for a moment basking in their heat.

'Not long though.'

He smiled and her heart melted all over again. He was a good man. A damned fine man, with demons. But then, didn't everyone have something? It just meant he had faced and fought and lived. Scars, even mental ones, were proof of survival.

'You did well back there, with Ashley.'

'We both did. I mean, it wasn't as if there was a lot we could do to actually help, but I hope we made them less panicked at least. I could tell you were thinking the same thing as me—get her the hell down the mountain.'

'Aye. We did good.'

'Yes.' She ran her fingers down his cheek. 'Here's to us.'

'To us.' Then his lips were on hers and all the emotion of the last few hours was infused in his kiss. He hauled her against him, not gently but with a need her body matched. There was no denying this. She was his and she wanted him to be hers. Everything they did together seemed to deepen the connection between them; she was falling harder and faster.

He tightened his grip around her and she held onto him, not wanting to let him go.

After a few minutes she became aware less of his amazing mouth and the hum of the wind in her ears and more aware of another kind of hum.

Abruptly, she pulled out of his arms. 'Did you hear something?'

'What?'

'I think it's my cell phone. Wait, let me look. It might be Mark, about Ashley. Or one of the paramedics or someone… I hope she's okay. And the baby.' Abbie shoved her hand into the bottom of her bag and pulled out her phone. Texts, so many texts. And missed calls. She scanned down the messages, her heart in her throat. 'She's in labour. She's been in labour for...'

'Well, they'll probably do a Caesarean just to get the baby out and then put her in an induced coma until they can get the blood pressure—'

'Not Ashley. *Emma*. Emma's in labour.' There were messages spanning back to when they'd started the walk. 'Well over an hour. Oh, damn. Damn and blast. *My* baby's coming and I'm up a stupid mountain trying to prove a point.'

And having the best kiss of her life.

Flinging the pack onto her back, she turned around and looked down the path. An hour's walking. A gondola, then a drive. She was going to miss the birth of her baby. How could she have done this?

How would she help Emma with a broken wrist? How would she hold her child?

Cal was looking at her as if he'd been punched in the gut. 'It's a bit early?'

'Yes. Yes. It's early, Cal,' she snapped, but couldn't help it. She needed to go. She shouldn't have even been here. 'Too early. She's not due for another few weeks. Oh, God, I hope they're okay. She must be going mad, wondering where I am.'

She fired back a text.

On my way. Don't you dare give birth without me!

Emma replied.

I've got my legs crossed, but I don't know how long I can do that for.

We'll be there as soon as we can.

We?

Me and Cal.

Emma fired back almost immediately:

Interesting...

Not interesting. Confusing.

'Come on. We've got to hurry.'

'Stop. Wait a second.' He was frustratingly slow all of a sudden. 'What did we talk about before? Going down is always tricky. One bad footstep and you're going to go head over heels. Take it easy.'

'Take it easy? Really? This baby is the only good thing in my life. It's the only good thing that came out of Michael dying. I promised Emma I'd be with her every step of the way, and here I am with you instead of with her.'

And yet, she wouldn't have given any of today up. Meeting Cal had been the best thing that had happened to her in a very long time. Today had been hugely emotional and intimate and the more she got to know him, the more he was chipping away at her heart. Coming up here had been her idea, not his. She'd wanted to trick him into facing his demons but here she was, facing hers instead.

'Look, I didn't mean that the way it sounded. I really didn't. Today has been so, so lovely. I'm just scared I'm going to miss one of the most important moments of my life. I have to be there. I have to go for my baby. Now.'

CHAPTER TWELVE

'OF COURSE YOU DO. And I'm going to get you there safely, okay?' Cal took her by the arm and made her stand still. 'If you start getting het up you might hurt yourself.'

Or worse. He knew how that went; getting emotional only made things less controllable.

'I can't imagine anything would make me hurt as badly as I do now, to be honest.' She shook her arm out of his grasp, but he made sure she was steady and not at risk of falling.

It was starting to rain now, to add to the mess. He had to take some control here. He couldn't stay. He couldn't be the father, or her lover, he couldn't walk into that labour room and help, or witness the birth of her child. But he could make sure she got there safely at least. 'I'm going to go first, okay, to set the pace I think we can safely go at. You will not run down this hill in the rain. Do you hear me?'

Her nostrils flared but she nodded. 'Yes.'

'You'll be no good to your baby or to Emma with two broken limbs or a damaged back.'

'Okay. Okay. Yes, I know. Just make sure your pace is fast.'

The path became slippery underfoot and her mood became equally dangerous.

And he knew she was blaming him.

And she was right to.

If she hadn't met him none of this would have happened. If she'd met some other man she could have a real future with, she wouldn't be grasping for little bits of joy or trying to prove to him that he could do things he was afraid of.

But she had met him, a man who already had enough responsibility and couldn't take any more on, who couldn't change his life to fit hers, no matter how much he wanted to.

He stopped to check she was okay, but she rushed past him and he let her. Because how could he stop her rushing towards the one thing she deserved more than anything—a future?

He watched the sway of her ponytail and the clip of her feet and his heart clenched like a fist.

He wanted to take her on. He wanted to stay. He wanted to be a father to her child.

He wanted to love her. He wanted her to be his responsibility.

Maybe he already did love her.

He tried to fathom it out. And every which

way he turned he couldn't ignore the fact that he was falling for her. Loving her.

Because who the hell brought someone a Christmas tree if they didn't love them even just a little bit?

Trouble was, he didn't think it was just a little bit. He thought it might be a whole lot.

Could be. If he stayed.

He groaned inwardly and upped his pace. It was a hell of a mess all round. And letting her in had been the most stupid thing he'd ever done. Almost.

The gondola ride and journey back to town were made in silence, save for the incessant tap of Abbie's good fingers on the dashboard as he pulled the car into a parking space at the hospital. She'd wanted to drive but he hadn't let her.

'I can absolutely drive. I know the roads better than you,' she'd railed at him.

But he'd climbed into the driver's seat and refused to move. 'You have an arm in a cast—how the hell can you grip the steering wheel?'

'How will I hold my baby? Or help Emma? I don't know, but I'm damned sure I will. So I can drive too.'

'Like hell.' And he'd gunned the engine and driven like a maniac, but it still wasn't fast enough for Abbie. Her body was coiled and tense, ready to jump and spring at any moment.

'Let's go through ED. That's the quickest route to the lifts.' She pushed him out of the car, assuming he was going to go with her. Once outside she took him by the hand and all but dragged him through the emergency department. Excitement rippled over her, as if someone had given her the best birthday present ever—and yet it was laced with trepidation. Fear. Panic.

As they rushed past ED Mission Control she paused briefly to speak to Nixon, one of the doctors. 'Hey, did you hear? Emma's having contractions.'

'Yes. She's up in Maternity. Her waters broke while she was here, working. Give her my regards, will you?' The doctor nodded hello at Cal and he nodded back, still unsure what the hell he was doing here. He should have just dropped her off. He was going to be no use up there; Emma wouldn't want him in the room.

But he couldn't let go of Abbie's hand. It was as if his body was clinging to the very last moments, to the last touch before it was prepared to let her go.

'Sure will, Nixon. Bye.' Abbie's face crumpled a little and she bit her bottom lip. 'I hope she's okay.'

'She'll be fine.' Cal squeezed her hand and she looked up at him, registering he was still there, still holding on, still marching along with her.

'Oh, Callum, my head's all over the place.'

'I'm not surprised. It's been a big day. A lot's happened.' So much.

The hospital had been transformed to a Christmas wonderland at some point over the last few days. Streamers zigzagged across the ceilings and someone had sprayed fake snow onto every window. There was a huge Christmas tree in Reception, and tinny Christmas music filled the air. It felt like another world. He thought about the real snow that was awaiting him in Duncraggen. So many thousands of miles away.

And of his brother who needed him. And how much Cal wanted to be there to look after him, and here to look after an amazing woman and her baby.

So much had happened. Too much for his poor, pathetic heart.

She gave him a sad smile as she pressed the lift call button. 'I can't believe it was this morning…that we…wow, Cal.' There were tears shimmering in her eyes. 'It's all muddling up. I didn't want it to be like this. I wanted… I don't know what I wanted. I'm going to be a mum and we just made love… I'm so confused. I have so many feelings. I don't think I'm making sense.'

Always so honest, putting his feelings into words for him. He tugged her against him, his heart contracting into a tight, fierce ball. Because, she was right. None of it made sense. How could it? It was all muddled. He needed to make things clear for her. For himself. He pulled away from her. 'Abbie, I'm going to just drop you up there on the ward, okay? You understand? I'm not going to stay.'

The lift pinged and the doors slid open. She jumped in and jabbed the seventh-floor button. 'Come on.' She looked back at him, confusion in her eyes. 'Wait…you mean…you're not coming in to see her?'

'No. You don't need me there. This is private. This is your family and your time. You don't need me.'

'I bloody well do.' Then she seemed to join up the dots of his thinking and her eyes grew wide. She tugged him into the empty lift just as the doors started to close. 'Oh, no. No. Don't do this right now, Cal. I haven't got time to even think about this. I can't just say goodbye and this be the end. Not of us. Not like this.'

He shrugged, his heart fracturing as his arms strained to hold her again, but he managed to control himself. 'We both knew it was going to happen, Abbie. Some time.'

'Not now, though. Please come with me. I want you there. You…you feel like family.'

How could he break her heart so swiftly?

Because he loved her, and it was best for both

of them if this ended now. He loved her. Dammit. He loved her and was going to lose her. 'But I'm not family, Abbie. I can't be. It's best if we don't get even more involved. I can't watch your friend give birth to your baby—that's not something I should be there for. I hardly know her. This is your time. Yours and Emma's.'

And Michael's.

Fourth floor. The door swished open. There was no one there.

She shook her head again, jabbed the seventh-floor button one more time and paced to the other side of the lift. 'No! I can't believe... I don't know what I believed. That somehow we'd make it through this. That somehow we'd make it work, Cal. You and me, we'd make it work.'

How could they? He pulled her to face him, felt the lurch in his gut and knew it had nothing to do with the lift jerking upwards. 'You'll have everything you want right here. And, what's more, you need to concentrate on Emma. Not me, or us, or whatever we just did.'

She blinked quickly. 'We made love, Callum.'

'Aye, we did.' It was the most amazing thing he'd ever done. *She* was the most beautiful thing he'd ever known. A huge weight pushed on his chest. There was absolutely no way he could stay and watch her hold her child and not be part of it.

She didn't need him here and, hell, he couldn't bear to be here and not be able to hold her again, not be able to make love to her. Not be able to be part of this. For ever. He had to cut loose.

His fingers went automatically to that crazy lock of hair that always fell differently from the rest and he wound it round his fingers. So soft. So strong. Like her. 'Your family is the most important thing to you, Abbie. Mine is to me too, and I have to be in Scotland. If we spend any more time together it'll just make things harder in the end. You need to focus on your baby and your new life. You'll forget me soon enough, when you're up to your arms in nappies and baby poop.'

'I don't think I'll ever forget you, Cal.'

Aye, she was imprinted on his heart, branded there, and there was no way he'd forget her. Ever.

The lift doors pinged open before he could say any more and they stepped into the very busy maternity corridor. Little children raced back and forth laughing, new mums waved goodbye to visitors. New dads clutching fresh bright flowers and balloons wandered around with tired, proud grins.

They found a nurse aide who pointed them to the labour suite and soon they were standing outside Emma's room.

Abbie went to open the door but he tugged

her hand gently. It was time to go. To actually take that step away. To give her the space she needed for her family. For her future, without him. 'Good luck, then, Abbie.'

I love you.

'No. No. No.' *Don't go,* her eyes pleaded. But then they flicked to the ward door and he knew he had to go right now, make it easy for her to leave him behind.

'Have the very best life, wee lassie.' If he faltered one step he might say or do something that had huge ramifications for them all. He had to go. He had to walk away. But first he ran his thumb over her lip—because he loved to do it. And knew she loved it too. He watched her eyes mist and saw the curl of her hand as it came towards him. He couldn't let her touch him, couldn't let her hold him.

He stepped away.

Her lip was trembling. 'Will you wait for me, Cal? Somewhere? Downstairs? In ED? The café? Please? Somewhere? I'll come down...soon. I don't know when... I don't know...when I know what's happening.' She looked bereft and his heart hurt; he'd done that to her. 'You will be there, won't you? When I come down?'

'Aye,' he whispered, hoping she wouldn't hear, or believe him.

Because they both knew he wouldn't be.

* * *

'Hey, there. Where's the hero of the hour?'
Emma was sitting up in bed, and across her belly
were tapes that fed to a monitoring machine. She
looked like a Christmas present all wrapped up.

Abbie had barely had time to wipe her eyes,
never mind find her happy voice. She'd watched
him walk away and prayed he'd look back, turn
back. *Come back.* But he'd done none of those
things. Her gaze had followed him the length of
the corridor, his confident swagger a little less
sure than normal. His shoulders had sagged. And
her heart had broken.

Because even though she'd known it was going
to happen she hadn't expected it to be so soon.
She hadn't expected to feel this much.

She hadn't expected to love him this hard.

And she did. Her eyes filled with tears, so she
busied herself looking at Emma's charts and trying to speak through a throat that was full and
raw. She loved him. And he was leaving her.
Right when she needed him most.

But that was pure selfishness, really. She
needed him, but she was asking far too much.
'Hey, gorgeous girl. Couldn't wait just a little
bit longer?' Her heart felt as if it were twisting
against her ribcage. 'Er… Callum, do you mean?
He's gone.'

'Oh. As in…gone home? Or *gone* gone?'

'Gone downstairs. But very likely gone altogether.' Abbie cleared her throat and dug deep for her smiley voice. 'You seem very happy given you're in labour.'

'This is baby number two. I know what to expect. Plus, there's a lot to be said for gas and air.' Emma patted the bed. 'Come and sit down and talk to me. You look bloody awful and you're not the one in a hospital bed. What the hell happened, hun?'

I fell in love. He broke my heart.

'You're in labour, my lovely friend, let's focus on that. On you and the baby. How did it start? How do you feel? How long have we got? Isn't it a bit early?'

'I'll tell you all that soon enough. We're going to be here for a few hours yet, I think.' But there was no getting past this. Emma was a terrier when it came to interrogation. 'You have probably about four minutes before the next contraction hits. I need some distraction, so talk. Or I'll scream the place down. Talk, woman.'

Abbie took a deep breath. She would say this once, get it out, then not mention him again. 'It hurts. I'm hurting all over again. But somehow this is almost worse than Michael, because he didn't have a choice, but Callum does. I do.' But how could you choose between families and their needs? She pressed her hand to her mouth to stop herself from crying, but it didn't seem to do much good. Tears began to drip onto the green hospital blanket leaving bleak circles. 'He said family was more important and that we didn't need him here. I knew it was going to happen. I just didn't think it'd hurt so much. I just hoped we'd have a bit more time. A lot more time.'

'You love him.' Abbie had expected Emma to be irritated by this, but she wasn't. She linked her fingers into Abbie's. 'I'm so sorry. I shouldn't have encouraged you to have a Highland fling. I should have known you'd fall for him.'

'How? Why?'

'What's not to like about the man? He's your Mr Perfect.'

Yes. 'This isn't helping. Let's talk about the baby. The plan. Right, so Rosie's staying at school until her uncle picks her up—'

'Coward. Yes, the plan's going fine. My bag was in my car, as we discussed, so Nixon went and got it for me. Which was kind of him.' Emma ran her hand over her stomach and the monitor printout started to jump. Another contraction was building. One step closer to holding her baby.

'Yes, it was.' Abbie still hadn't mentioned that weird conversation with Nixon earlier this week and now she definitely wouldn't. Not the right time or place. 'Yes, let's distract each other. Are we sure we're happy with Michaela for a girl and Michael for a boy?'

'Your call. If you want to honour your husband, then that's great. Really great. If you want to move on, then that's good too. This is your baby.'

'*Our* baby. Yours and mine and Rosie's. A collective effort for one very longed-for child.' She looked at her beautiful friend wince in pain, and wondered how she could have agreed to put her through this, but knowing she'd have done the same if given a chance. Because families did come first and, above everything, Emma and Abbie were sisters in everything except blood.

She wanted to ask her how she felt about handing the baby over after all of this, but couldn't go there. It was something they'd have to deal with at the time. Nothing could prepare them for that moment. She stroked Emma's hair back from her face.

But Emma leaned forward, frowning. 'What's the matter? Why are you looking at me like that? Like *I* just broke your heart?'

'I'm not. It's not… I'm not.' Abbie made herself smile.

But Emma was starting to tense with the pain. 'Am I imagining it, then? When I said it was your baby, you jumped right in and said *ours*. It's not ours. It's yours, Abbie. What's the matter? Don't you think—? Oh, my God! You don't think I'm going to give it to you, do you?'

This.

On top of Cal leaving. It was too much. One moment Abbie had almost had everything and then…so close to losing everything. 'I just thought… I couldn't give my baby away. I don't know how you can.'

For a moment, Abbie thought Emma was going to growl at her, but her eyes softened and she covered Abbie's plaster-casted hand with hers. 'Oh, honey. I thought you were being a bit weird about it. Every time we talked about this moment you referred to the baby as ours, as if you were suggesting I wanted it and you were trying to keep me sweet. Don't worry, okay? Whatever happens, I will give you this baby. I love it, yes, of course I do. It's been inside me for so long I've definitely grown attached. But, not to the point of wanting to keep it all for me.'

'So, you're okay about handing it over? Are you sure?' Relief rolled through Abbie; she'd been secretly so worried that at the end of these nine months she'd still have no baby to call her own. 'I should have said something. I'm sorry. I should have trusted you more.'

'Yes, you should have. Or we should have talked more about it. I thought you believed me,

but I can imagine how you've been worrying. I
know what you're like, Abbie Cook.'

'I heard some women gossiping at work and it
sent my head into a spin.' Seemed that happened
a lot these days.

Emma's eyes closed for a moment and she
seemed to be controlling her breathing; either
riding the contraction or just pretending to feel
better about things than she wanted to let on...
Abbie would never really know. 'I am absolutely
one hundred per cent certain I do not want to
keep your baby. I have one of my own, thanks,
a sweet five-year-old, and I'm done with nappies and toddler tantrums. Plus, to be honest, I'm
a little over heartburn and sleepless nights too.
And this, yes, this, lying on a bed in agony...is
not exactly fun. I don't want to be pregnant again
for a very long time. If ever... No. Never again!'
Her grip tightened around Abbie's bruised fingers. 'Okay. Here we go. This. Bloody. Hurts.'

'I know. I know. I'm so sorry. I wish it was
me. You know I can't thank you enough for this,
but...can you hold the other hand, please? This
one is damaged enough.'

'Sorry. Sorry. Not sorry. Pass me the gas and
air.' Emma screwed her eyes closed as Abbie
ran round to the end of the bed and grabbed the
cylinder and mouthpiece. Once back at Emma's
side she let her friend have some long puffs and

then stroked her back. 'You're doing so well. So very well.'

Emma puffed out as she breathed through the pain. 'Things haven't got interesting yet. We'll see. Now, no more talk about who's going to bring up this baby, okay? He's yours. She's yours. All yours. With love.'

'Okay. Thank—'

'Hello!' A midwife came into the room. 'How are we doing?'

'Managing.' With a grunt, Emma hauled herself up the bed and Abbie rearranged pillows, feeling useless.

The midwife looked at the monitor printout and nodded. 'We can take this off now. Everything is fine there. I just need to check on a couple more things, see how well you're dilating. You want your friend here?'

'No. She's going to the shop. I'd like some magazines and mints, please.' Tired eyes looked over. She was hurting but pretending she was fine. Story of Emma's life. 'Go. You never know who you might meet down there.'

Cal had long gone, Abbie was sure. 'Okay. Don't do anything while I'm gone.'

'I wouldn't dream of it. See if you can find him. Talk to him. Phone him. Tell him how you feel.'

'Why?'

'Because this is one chance you won't have again.'

'But, what about… Scotland? He lives in Scotland.'

Emma was being draped with a towel and the midwife was about to get serious, but Emma flashed a smile that was filled with love and a positivity that actually hurt Abbie's heart. 'We'd get by. You saved me from myself, Abbie. You helped me when I had nowhere to go with that bastard of a man trying to hurt me. I owe you. So what's a few thousand miles between friends?'

'I wouldn't go.' She couldn't. She couldn't leave her friend, her family.

Besides, he hadn't asked. He understood. Which made it all so much harder.

One last weak word as the midwife snapped on gloves. 'Mints?'

'Oh. Yes. Sorry. I'll go now.' Abbie tiptoed out and pulled the door behind her, pausing for time. Because she didn't want to go downstairs and see that he wasn't there.

CHAPTER THIRTEEN

CAL HAD MANAGED to keep a lid on things in the hospital, but out on the lake path he let rip; running at top speed for as long as he could push his body, until every muscle screamed for relief. Then doubling up as he hauled as much oxygen as he could into his lungs.

He'd done the right thing. He had. But everything felt wrong. Everything was wrong. He should have stayed with her. He should have told her how he felt.

But then what? What good would that have done? It would have just mired them deeper into a situation they couldn't fix.

The lake was so calm today it was in direct contrast to his insides. He needed to run again. And fast. But, in perfect, typical timing, his phone rang.

Cal was not in the mood to talk to his brother, but every time he saw the name *Finn* flash up on his display his heart thundered. Emergency? Depression? Who was watching him? 'You okay?'

'Yes. Fine.' A long sigh. 'What are you doing?'

Cal fought for enough breath to manage more than two words. 'Running. By the lake. Trouble sleeping?'

'Aye. The usual.'

'Maybe you need to do more exercise during the day, Finn. Tire yourself out physically, you know.' Although right now it didn't seem to be working for Cal. He felt painfully, hopelessly alive.

There was a pause. 'What's wrong?'

'Nothing.' Cal walked to a lakeside bench. The same bench he'd been at when she'd run past him and challenged him to a race. *Damn.* Everything about Queenstown would be tinged with memories of her. *Good job you're leaving soon.*

'Look, pal, you're my brother. I know when there's something wrong. Your voice is flat. You're not your usual sunny self.' Finn laughed. Because Cal hadn't ever been described as sunny and certainly never by his brother. 'What's got your goat this time? Job? Me? A woman?'

There was a catch in Cal's throat and he wheezed. 'Nothing.'

'Ah. Woman.'

'None of your business.'

'Spill the beans, man. I have all night, literally.' As if to prove his point Finn stretched out on the sofa and Cal got a glimpse of the lounge. Tidy. Neat. Clean. Finn had shaved. Wow, things had taken a turn for the better, just from yesterday. There was something about him that was different too. He was…lighter somehow. His mood was better. Hope underpinned his voice.

Unlike Cal's. 'I don't feel much like talking.'

There was another pause. Finn ran a hand over his jaw and smiled. Another unusual thing. 'That's not like you. I remember that long night on the ridge and how you blathered on and on and on. I couldn't shut you up.'

'I was trying to keep you awake. To keep you…you know…with me.' They'd never talked about that night before. Never gone there. He wasn't minded to go there now either.

'And you did. And you have, many times since, Cal. I know. I'm grateful. I mean it.' Finn actually looked a little embarrassed. 'Really. I owe you. So talk again now.'

'Ach, it's nothing.' It was everything. But if he started he might just never stop.

When had he said that before? Ah yes, to her. And she'd made him talk and he had and he'd felt better. She'd made him better, had helped to heal some wounds.

'What's her name?'

'Abbie.' There was a fist of pain under his ribcage just saying it. He rubbed to make it go away. It didn't.

Finn's eyebrows rose. 'And what's the problem with this Abbie?'

Where to start? He couldn't be in two places at once. Didn't know if he had enough space in his head or his heart for her and a baby when he was already brimful of responsibilities. Plus, the distance. So many problems. But his subconscious seemed to be one step ahead as he blurted out, 'She's having a baby.'

'What?' First time in a while he'd seen his brother's eyes shine. 'Way to go! You wee randy devil.'

Cal kept a small smile to himself, because no way would anyone believe him if he tried to explain the whole story. 'No. Not mine.'

'But you want it to be yours, right? You want her?'

'Aye.' More than anything. A huge admission, but yes. He wanted her and this baby.

'So what's stopping you?'

You. Me. Fear. Duty. He cleared his throat; no point in going there. 'How's everything going?'

Finn raised his hand and pointed to the clean room. 'Better, so much better. It's about time I got my act together and smartened things up—

so don't go thinking I miss you. I've got news too. The old boss said I could go back one day a week in the new year. See how I go.'

'Back to work?' Cal didn't know how he felt about that. He thought for a moment. A ball of heat filled his chest. Proud, actually. A bit of trepidation. Feeling his brother slipping away a little. In a good way. Cutting some ties. 'Good. That's great. You'll have to sort your sleeping out, though.'

'I'm working on it.'

It was something they could work on together. 'Okay, well, we can make an appointment with the doctor and talk it through. When I'm home. I've been reading up on sleep routines—'

'Leave it, Cal. I'm managing.' His brother's jaw had set. Not a good sign.

'I'll see you on the nineteenth. We can talk more about it then.'

'Ah—yes. About that.'

'I've got a shuttle booked from the airport and Maggie can get some food in. Don't worry about anything.'

Finn's hands were palm up towards the screen. *Stop. Stop. Stop.* 'Enough, Cal. Stop it. Stop.' He scrubbed a hand over his hair, the sheepish look coming back. 'Thing is…' He took a big deep breath and blew out slowly. 'Thing is… I don't want you to come back.'

What the hell? 'Why not?'

'I know you feel responsible for what happened, but you're not. We made a stupid mistake and we don't both need to spend the rest of our lives paying for it.'

'But I said—'

Finn nodded. 'Yes, I know what you said. I heard every word through that freezing night. Your voice kept me alive Goddammit. *You* kept me alive.' He actually did sound grateful and humbled, not angry. Even a little choked up. 'And thank you, but all of this…living-with-me thing…it's too much. You can't put your life on hold for me in some sort of penance.'

There was no question or debate; he had to look after his brother. 'It's not a penance.'

'It's a pain in the arse, is what it is. I can't do anything without you telling me how to do it. I know it's just your way, but I need to live my own life.' Now he was back to his normal annoying self. *Brothers.* 'Oh, and I'm sorry, but I have a confession to make.'

'What?' Cal's interest was piqued along with his mood.

Finn did that funny grimace men did when they didn't want to say something but knew they had to. A sort of *sorry, mate but…tough love* kind of thing. 'It was me who spoke to your boss about an exchange to New Zealand in the first place, and he agreed you needed some space. It was me who paid for the airfare—we didn't get nearly as much as we wanted to by fundraising. I needed you out of my hair. I needed you to learn how to live without guilt. Everyone else just helped with the organisation and amped up the idea to make you go.'

The last few months had been a set-up? 'But I wanted to help you. I still do. It's my job—you're my brother. You're family.'

'Aye. And I still will be whether you live here or in New Zealand or Timbuktu. So—you're free to do what you want. Go wild, have fun. Or… you know. Go get her.'

'I can't stop worrying about you just because you want me to.' Depression sometimes came back. Cal wanted to be there in case it did.

But Finn shook his head. 'I'm fine. I'm getting stronger every day. Stop using me as an excuse not to live your life.'

'I'm not. What about the Search and Rescue? My job.'

'Excuses. Just excuses, trying to find reasons why not instead of, *why the hell not*? I should know, I've been doing the same for long enough. You're scared to commit to anyone or anything in case it goes wrong. But look at me—things do go wrong, but we survive. We survive, Cal, and we live. Time to face reality and make the most of it.'

'Well, now I want whatever it is that you've been taking.' But Finn was right. Cal had worn his duties as a shield, held his job and his brother up as reasons why he couldn't give his heart to Abbie. But she had it anyway, in the palm of that damaged hand of hers. He'd been afraid of letting her in, because the simple truth of it was that he hadn't thought he had enough space in his life to take on more. But at what cost? Losing her altogether? Losing the chance of happiness? A life? A family of his own? He was losing all that by not even considering any other way.

Could he let Finn go, though? Could he stand aside and watch him falter? He wanted so much for him to be well—maybe this was a first shaky step of actually allowing him to be.

They had daily conversations across the world as it was—nothing there needed to change. And he could still be a brother and a husband and…a father. Something hopeful bloomed in his gut. 'Er… Finn, you know that skiing trip?'

'Aye?'

He needed to get back to the hospital and tell her. He hoped she'd be willing to have him in her life. Was it too late? Had he already hurt her enough by leaving her right when she'd needed him most? Would she even want him, when she had her own little family already? He had to try at least. 'I don't think I can make it after all.'

His brother grinned. 'Well, thank God for that.'

'You're doing so well. So bloody well. I'm so proud of you. Keep breathing, that's it. Pant. Pant.' Abbie gripped Emma's hand and let her squeeze as hard as she wanted to. For the last two hours they'd been in a tight, half-lit cocoon of contractions and hand-holding and tears as the contractions had become closer and stronger.

But now things were really starting to happen. The midwife peered over Emma's legs. 'Good girl. The baby's crowning. I can see the head.'

'Oh, my God. Oh! This is it. This is real.' There was a moment when Abbie didn't know whether to laugh or cry, so she did both.

And Emma joined in. But hers were mixed with screams and grunts. 'I'm...so glad...you didn't miss this.'

'It's thanks to Callum that I'm here at all. He drove—'

He drove me here. He made sure I was safe. He made me love him.

He was missing out. His loss. She couldn't believe he'd walked away like that. Or how much she'd hurt at the thought of him not being around. She didn't want to think of waking up tomorrow and not seeing him. Or being at work hoping for the sound of his voice that would make her day so much better.

She didn't want to think of Christmas Day. For so long she'd been looking forward to Christmas and now it felt tarnished without him. But she couldn't change the fact he didn't want to be here, couldn't be here.

She pushed thoughts of him as far away from here and now as she could. She wiped her friend's face with a cool damp flannel, wishing there was more she could do to help. 'You're amazing, Em. Not long to go.'

'Whoa…! I need to push. Right now!' And with that Emma took a huge breath and groaned and squeezed and pushed and pushed.

And Abbie watched and waited and worried.

'Good. Excellent. Yes…yes. Here! A girl. You've got a darling girl. All fingers and toes accounted for. She's gorgeous.' The midwife handed a squirming, wriggling, waxy baby into Abbie's waiting hands, but she couldn't hold it properly and her gut contracted. She dug deep and found enough strength to hold her long enough for one falling-in-love rush. 'Here. Put her on Emma's tummy.'

'You want to cut the cord?' The midwife again.

Scissors were placed in Abbie's good hand.

Which was shaking as much as her heart was thumping. 'Oh, yes. Yes, please.'

And then the room was filled with fledgling wails and Emma's little sniffles as she stroked the baby's down-covered back, and Abbie snipped. And they were all in tears. Because this really was the most beautiful thing. The best gift any-one could ever give.

'Let me help you.' The midwife lifted the baby up and went to put her on Emma's chest, but Emma shook her head.

'Give her to Abbie. Give her to her mum.'

Abbie couldn't fight tears any more. *Mum.* She was a mum. A mum. Wow. 'Are you sure? You don't want to hold her first?' There were tears streaming down Emma's face and Abbie didn't know if it was a good thing or not. 'Do you... how do you feel? Is everything okay?'

Wiping her face with the back of her hand, Emma smiled. 'I'm fine. Really. Just hormonal, and emotional. And I just love the look on your face. You look so, so happy. It's a big thing, being a mum. I know. I already am one. Now you are too.'

Then Abbie was sitting down and holding the most precious, the most adorable, the cutest baby, in the whole world. And yes, she was bi-ased, but she didn't care. It was true. She looked deep into those big eyes and her heart was lost.

For ever. This was it. Hopelessly in love. Funny, how that could happen twice in one day. This one, though, this one would stay for a while at least. She looked up at her best friend. 'Thank you. Thank you. I just want to make sure you're okay with this.'

Emma sniffed and sat up a little, trying to make herself comfortable after her ordeal. 'Of course I'm okay with it. She was never mine to begin with, Abbie. She's yours. All yours. Look, she's got your eyes.' Emma looked straight into Abbie's eyes and blinked quickly. 'Oh. She's so beautiful.'

'Of course she is. And very few tears, look, she's just quietly watching. Such dainty fingers and toes. So graceful. Right. I've decided, I'm going to call her Grace.'

'Not Michaela?'

A wave of sadness rippled through Abbie, and she let it go. 'That can be her middle name. I don't want to feel sad every time I call to her. She deserves her own name. And I need to move forward. In so many ways. This is a new start. My new family of two.' Abbie squeezed her friend's arm. 'I don't know how the hell I'm ever going to repay you.'

'For what? Being a friend? You've done it a thousand times over since we were muddy-kneed with toothless smiles, and nothing but trouble.'

With a sigh, Emma lay back against her pillows. 'Just love her, okay?'

'I already do. I'm besotted. Completely. And I love you, and Rosie, with all my heart.'

And it was true. So very true. But there was one corner of her almost full heart that would never be the same, that would never heal. Because Callum wasn't here to share in all of this.

He found her in the nursery. With her back to him, she was standing over a crib whispering softly to a baby.

A boy? A girl? He couldn't tell from here. It was swaddled in a white sheet and just stirring from sleep, its tiny arms and legs jerking in the air.

She leant in and twisted her wrist to pick it up. Flinched. Twisted again at a different angle.

No way was she a quitter.

Not like him. One sniff of emotional trouble and he was off.

Not any more. 'You want some help?' He kept his voice low, but even then she jumped and turned round.

'Cal?' There was pride glowing in her eyes, but caution too. And love. She was scared. She'd been through so much. He'd hurt her, he knew, and she wasn't going to let him do it again. She pressed her lips together and shook her head. 'I'm okay. I can manage. We can manage, thanks.'

'Do you want to sit down and I'll lift her? Him? Into your arms?'

'Her. She's a girl. Grace. My daughter.'

My daughter. It was a swift blow to his heart. He'd chosen to walk away from this? A fool. Stupid really was his middle name.

'Hey, wee bairn. Abbie, she's so beautiful.' There was a fierce possessive streak in him; he knew that very well. Finn had called him on it and Abbie had too. But it was because he cared. Cared deeply and wanted to protect the people he loved from every potential harm. And right now that same streak was running through him as he looked into the black button eyes of this little scrap of life. He wanted to be a part of this. He wanted this child to be his daughter.

He choked that all back—it was too much to think that she'd refuse him, refuse this. But he wouldn't blame her if she did. 'And Emma? How is she?'

'Sad, I think, but she won't admit it. She did so well. So very well, but she's tired now and resting. I take over from here, so I'm on a steep learning curve.'

'So let me help.' Without discussing it further, he took her hand and sat her down in one of the large, soft feeding chairs. She looked exhausted and this was just the beginning. Every part of him craved to look after her. He wanted to hold her—and the baby—and keep them safe.

But she was still guarded. 'Why are you here?'

'Two things.' He went with the easier one first. 'I've just been talking to Nixon. He's had word that Ashley's okay... Ashley, from the gondola, with pre-eclampsia... She's still very sick, but they're confident she'll pull through. And baby's in NICU, but doing fine.'

'Thank goodness. I was so worried.' She looked over at Grace, who was starting to make little chirruping noises, and her eyes misted. She pressed a fist to her chest. 'I couldn't imagine...'

'Don't. Don't even think about it. You want to hold her?'

There was a smile. 'Yes. All the time.'

'I don't blame you. Wait there.' His heart was racing as he bent to pick little Grace up, but it just about melted as she wrapped her tiny fingers round his thumb. *This.* This was what he craved. There was something raw and thick in his throat. 'Here you go. She's beautiful. Like you.'

'Callum. I can't...not here.' She took the babe into her waiting arms and looked down at her with such tenderness that he didn't think he could hold himself together for much longer. He loved her and loved that child—a miracle that he could feel this way so quickly.

'So...' He wondered if he was making the same kind of face as his brother had a few hours ago. There were so many important things he had to say, he just didn't know if they'd come out right. 'I want you to know that I love you, Abbie. That I'm staying here, in Queenstown, indefinitely.'

'You love me? You...love me? You walked away, Cal. You walked away when I needed you.' Her eyes widened. 'Why the change of heart?'

He pulled a chair over to sit next to her. 'There was never a change of heart. I always wanted to stay. I just couldn't be in two places at once. I couldn't be a brother and a...partner...boyfriend.' *Family.* 'I couldn't give everything to everyone. At least, I didn't think I could. But I want to be here. With you. And little Grace. I want us to be a family.'

'And Finn?'

'He's fine. He's a lot better and I actually need to let him get on with his life the way he wants.'

'You've come a long way.' Abbie gave him a very gentle smile and placed her palm on his cheek the way she'd done so many times before. And it gave him some hope. 'It's a lovely thought. It really is.'

But... He could tell from her tone that there was a *but* coming. Hope faded.

'But how do I know you won't walk again?

How can I let you in when you might leave? You're a bit of a flight risk. Don't you have a ticket for home?'

She wasn't going to make this easy for him, and who could blame her? He grabbed his phone and showed her the airline app. The cancelled flight. Nothing booked, nothing planned, except staying here. On that point, he was absolutely certain. 'This is my home, Abbie. Here. With you and Grace, if you'll have me.'

His home. The words struck her chest in a hard blow. Abbie watched as he shoved his phone into his pocket and she started to believe that maybe this was the new fresh start she craved. Him. A man who had been through so much, who'd shown he was good and honourable by knowing his limits, by not making false promises. A man she loved hopelessly. 'We're a lot to take on, Cal. I know that. It's complicated and messy. It's a lot of responsibility.'

'Which I want. I want you, both of you. We'll make it work. *I'll* make it work.'

And his voice was so ardent and the passion in his face so honest and true she believed him. Almost. 'Grace deserves someone who'll stay around.'

'I intend to and I'll prove that to you every day. Just know that I love you, and that's never going to change.' He was leaning closer now, his mouth inches from hers, his eyes filled with love, and she could feel the tug into his arms. 'I want us to be a family, Abbie. And that means I want it all; the wedding, everything.'

'What? A wedding?' He really was serious. 'Is this…? A mother and a wife in one day! Are you asking me to marry you?'

'Aye. I suppose I am.' He ran his finger over her necklace and came to a halt when he connected with her wedding ring. Held his breath, his eyes capturing her gaze. 'Yes. Yes, I am asking you to be my wife. Marry me, Abbie?'

And she wanted so much to stay like this, feeling like this, being with him for the rest of her life. Placing her palm over his, she nodded, because words were just too hard to say through a throat so thick with emotion. And she was concentrating on not crying because that might wake the baby.

'Is that a yes?'

Not crying wasn't happening. She felt the first tear, then the rest roll down her cheeks. 'Yes. Of course. Yes! Oh, I love you, Callum.'

'I love you too. Both of you.'

And then he kissed her. A promise. For ever.

EPILOGUE

It was very early on Christmas morning, but Callum had been up for hours. He was standing by the Christmas tree, rocking his darling daughter, trying to get her to go back to sleep. He'd been the last to bed and up in the small hours and again now. At some point, they'd manage a whole night's sleep, but probably not for a few years. 'Shh, you'll wake Mummy.'

Abbie was watching from the doorway. Every time she saw that big strong man holding her tiny little daughter—their daughter—her heart pinged with a rush of love. 'Too late. I'm already awake.'

'Ach, sorry, love. We managed a nappy change and a feed but I think she wants entertaining.'

'Presents?' She looked over at the huge pile that had accumulated over the last few weeks. Gifts from her parents, from Emma's family. From work. And, of course, gifts from Callum. So many, too many.

But this was the best one: to watch him being a father to her child. To know he was staying. That he was part of her family. She didn't know if she'd ever felt so happy. 'No, we'll do presents when we get back. Now that we're all up, should we go now?'

'Aye. We're all dressed up in our Christmas best, aren't we?' He kissed Grace on both cheeks and secured her in her pushchair, grabbed the toys and entertainment, then wrapped Abbie into his arms. The place she always wanted to be. 'I love you. Did I ever tell you that?'

'I know you do. And I love you too. But hurry, or we'll be too late.'

Their route took them out through the botanical gardens and along the lake path. There weren't many other runners out so early, but they did pass some exhausted-looking parents with excited kids on sparkly new bikes and scooters, and they gave each other that tired grin that said, *happy*.

When they reached the bench, they unpacked, dialled and waited for him to answer. It was still Christmas Eve there and he was going out, so they didn't want to miss him.

'Hey, how's my beautiful girl doing?' Clearly, being soppy but pretending not to be ran in the family. Finn had been besotted with Grace and being an uncle from the minute he'd set eyes on her—distance didn't mean a thing with technology these days. 'It's snowing, look. This is snow, Gracie. This is Scotland at Christmas. Cold. Damp. But there's lots of whisky, so not too bad at all.'

'I think she's a little young for whisky, Finn.' But the little girl followed his smile and gurgled. Abbie grinned, snuggling into Callum's arms, her favourite place in the world. 'It's just how I imagined it would be. Magical. Look at this, Cal, your village really is like a film set. Isn't it beautiful?'

'Hmm? Beautiful? Yes. You are.' He kissed the back of her neck, then the side of her head. And she turned and kissed him full on the mouth.

'Hey, guys! Children watching!' Finn was shouting and laughing thousands of miles away. 'Please be mindful of our innocence.'

'Yeah, says the guy who was dating well before his older brother. Happy Christmas, Finn. Have a great one. And, please, be good.'

'I'm always good. I'm golden, mate. Happy Christmas, everyone.'

'Now, where were we?' With one sweep of his hand, Cal closed down the app. With a sweep of his other hand he'd picked up Grace and buckled her into her pushchair again. Then with both arms he wrapped Abbie into a hug.

'I think you'll find we were right here. Doing

this.' She kissed him hard, then pulled out of his arms. Ready to race. 'Last one back to the flat is a turkey.'

'Or cooks the turkey.'

'I'm definitely going to win, then.' But she didn't shoot off. Instead, she stopped, taking it all in. One minute to smell the roses. Two. Three. For ever. She gazed first at her man, then at her child…then out across the deep blue lake and the soaring mountain backdrop. Their first family Christmas.

No need to race any more. She'd already won.

* * * * *

Read on for the next great story in
THE ULTIMATE CHRISTMAS GIFT *duet*

HER NEW YEAR BABY SURPRISE
by Sue MacKay

And, if you enjoyed this story,
check out these other great reads
from Louisa George

TEMPTED BY HOLLYWOOD'S TOP DOC
HER DOCTOR'S CHRISTMAS PROPOSAL
TEMPTED BY HER ITALIAN SURGEON
A BABY ON HER CHRISTMAS LIST

All available now!